FREEDOM'S FLOW

1815: Raised in a convent, Ruby has been taken from its shelter to be placed in the service of Mr Sedgwick of Tilbury. Her new master is elusive, and the reason for her presence there seems a mystery. Meanwhile, Giles Marram has returned home from the wars to find much has changed — a beautiful maid has been moved into the Hall. But why is Marram's former captain seeking her out?

VALERIE HOLMES

FREEDOM'S FLOW

Complete and Unabridged

LINFORD
Leicester

First published in Great Britain in 2018

First Linford Edition
published 2018

A catalogue record for this book is available
from the British Library.

ISBN 978–1–4448–3652–3

Published by
F. A. Thorpe (Publishing)
Anstey, Leicestershire

Set by Words & Graphics Ltd.
Anstey, Leicestershire
Printed and bound in Great Britain by
T. J. International Ltd., Padstow, Cornwall

This book is printed on acid-free paper

1

Ruby watched the mighty waterway steadily filling the marsh trenches that had been marked out over centuries. Time and tide had brought many people up and down the great River Thames. It flowed in from the sea — or, as Ruby imagined, from the vast oceans — and continued on its way up to the ancient city of London and beyond. Undeterred by its meandering, trade continued today as it had for centuries: the skyline was dotted with sails on ships of all descriptions, steadily moving along. The backdrops of both the Kent hills and Essex marshes provided a fascinating surround to where all manner of businesses fared. To Ruby's young eyes, the ships' flags represented the whole world, whilst she stood there, rooted in time and place, only able to watch them drift by.

She leant against the stone wall of the

fort. Rather than feeling discomfort at the cold that passed through the fabric of her dress, chilling her body, she imagined she was absorbing some of its strength. The abandoned fortification was now her own castle, and she was there — waiting, always waiting, for her knight to come and rescue her from her new life of servitude.

The fort, so recently deserted, still seemed to resonate with the echoes of the many orders shouted within. Fanciful notion it was, but Ruby smiled, because notions were priceless and all of her own making.

'Ruby!' A distant call carried on the breeze.

Ruby sighed, surprised, for the voice was not that of Mrs Grambler, the cook of Yew Tree Hall, but a male one. Here she was, outside the walls of a fort, not locked within as she had been at the convent. Yet there were invisible walls in the Hall that, as a servant, she could not go beyond. So she still felt trapped. Even in her few peaceful moments there was someone searching her out. Who? She did not know. She possessed little enough in life — but at least her thoughts could be her own, if not her time.

'Ruby!' The voice grew louder and more determined as it rolled over the marshland that surrounded the south side of the Hall down to the fort, the edge of which fell into the mudflats of the river.

Still, she smiled, and tucked a wayward fiery auburn curl behind her ear without a sense of urgency. The call ignored, she was in good humour. Her memories of the enforced doctrines of her childhood were in the past: no more midnight prayers for her! Just long days of toil that ended with her going late to bed and early to rise; but many of the hours in between were apparently hers to dream away. So perhaps life here would not be that bad.

'Ruby!' The voice was no nearer or louder, but the snap it held carried to her ears like a whiplash, and this time she moved, conscience finally pricked.

3

She'd have to go back. Now, she realised that the deep and persistent voice belonged to Giles Marram, the blacksmith's son. Why he wanted her, she knew not. What was more, she did not want to find out. He was supposed to be a hero, returned from fighting Napoleon. Maisie, the kitchen-cum-housemaid, was full of gossip about him and what he had done; how he had brought Napoleon to his knees — almost! Whatever nonsense the woman talked, Ruby was not impressed with, because she was obviously besotted by the man's charm.

Standing straight, she gathered her shawl around her shoulders and turned her back to this place that she loved. The wind direction was changing, and brought with it a mixture of odours; she didn't care for that aspect of the river trade. The manufactories spilled their essence into its waters to send them out to sea as the river became tidal. Gone was the breath of fresh air that had stirred her imagination. She had heard the traders talk of the manufactories' big chimneys nearer the city. They sounded horrible. Imperfect and impure as life here was, it was hers.

'Ruby . . . ' The voice was drifting away. Good. Giles had missed her. He was handsome: his hair had a wave to it when wet, and dried with blonde lights amongst its sandy hues. She had only noticed when she happened to see him dip his head in a barrel of water at the back of his father's forge when she had arrived. The coach had halted to have a horseshoe checked. She had not realised just how much detail of the man she had taken in as he pulled on his shirt. Her eye had followed the form of his muscular chest from his throat, over his sculptured front, to the top of his broad leather belt. He was well-groomed and clean, considering this man was a tradesman. The few times she had seen him since, usually talking to Maisie in the garden when he brought something to the Hall, Ruby could see that he had a way with him that was friendly. Perhaps he had the eyes of the few eligible girls in the village. Maisie obviously yearned for him, but why should he be calling for Ruby and seeking her out?

She paused momentarily, watching a large packet going downriver, and wondered what it would be like to be upon one of them. There were many colliers; they were grim, but on one of the spectacular tall ships you could travel to new and exciting lands.

If only I could sail away and see new places. Follow the river's flow to even greater freedom. Ah, she loved that thought; but, as the sun was high in the sky, her time for daydreaming was gone.

She walked slowly along the curvature of the wall and peered over the fields to the grey building that overlooked the plain down to the fort, marsh and river. This was a quiet place: tucked away on the banks, amidst a myriad of runnels to the river where travellers passed by without a second glance her way. They would have noticed the old Tilbury Fort as they went by this battery. 'Hope', they called it, and here she would keep her own hope alive.

Ruby glanced apologetically to the ancient church behind her. Still, the God she had loved as a child had stopped listening to her when it was demanded she obeyed the rules of the sisters. So she stood up, head slumped, and returned to the path that led back to the Hall.

2

Giles had scoured the area. He doubled back, frustrated; she could not have been far away. He glanced at the battery and shrugged. No young lass would go to such a dangerous place. The area around it was no place for a woman. He knew Ruby often wandered around like a lost soul. He'd watched her, transfixed by her fine looks and free spirit, but she shouldn't be out on the marshes. It just wasn't safe. Not only could the land itself play tricks on the unsuspecting, but there were people who used the marshes who would take great joy in finding a beauty such as Ruby out on her own.

When he saw her in the distance, he followed and made sure that she didn't get lost or stuck. He knew the tidal paths like the back of his father's hand, having played on them as a child. He grinned because, as he had watched his father work, he must be more familiar with the other man's hands than his own.

Today, Giles was later than usual, and he had missed her ... missed seeing her in more ways than one. She was not like the other girls that were silly and flirty around him; Ruby looked through, or past, him as if he did not exist on the few times their paths crossed in the walled garden or after church. Why? He could not have offended her, yet she acted as if he had. This gnawed at and fascinated him equally.

The more she avoided him, the more he wanted to make her acknowledge him. However, she must stop going down by the fort. If the foolish girl had been so bold, then he would have to warn her to take care. If what he had overheard in the Bull Inn was true, she must stay well clear. How to make her do that without telling her what her ears should not hear? Giles could just walk away; if she gallivanted around on her own in such places, then she was open to danger by her own doing. But he did care, and care deeply. He would find a way for her to see and listen to him, and then she must obey his words. After all, she was just a young wench, wherever she came from; he was a man of the village, and knew a great deal more than she would ever be party to.

★   ★   ★

Cook was busy as usual, but she was also outside. Ruby's heart sank. She had stayed out far too long again. She approached quickly with what she hoped was a friendly smile on her face.

''Ere! Where've you been, you lazy baggage?' The voice of Cook bellowed across the small herb garden out the back of the Hall.

Ruby lifted her head high, and replied in a cheerful voice, 'Sorry, Cook. I've been watching the ships come and go.' Cook wasn't one to grizzle much, but when she did she could go on complaining for minutes at a time.

Cook shook her head. 'Girl, if you go off wandering and dreaming like that and are caught by the master, you're going to be seeing more than you'd like of ships and sailors — down at the docks! Be grateful you have a place here, for you is on very thin ice.' Cook shook her head.

'I've always wondered what the frost fares were like,' Ruby said with an impish smile; but then caught the shard of a icy glare and quickly continued, 'I was just wondering what it would be like to be really free, to sail off to see new places, like the travellers on those ships.' Ruby stared back down the track that led to the marshes. 'Can you imagine leaving this place — this life — and seeing the world?'

'Get that nonsense out of your head right now! Do you think them felons — poor sods! — that is being sent off to Australia wants to be on them ships?

Nor them poor heathens what've been traded in chains? Do you think they wanted to leave their homelands and kin? Nor even the hardworking hands that take coal up and down the rough seas to Newcastle or other foreign parts — what about all the men that went to war — or them that were pressed into HM Navy, without even a chance to say their farewells . . . '

'No, Cook, I suppose not,' Ruby cut in before Cook's head exploded with all the power of her heartfelt rant. 'But they're all going somewhere, and I'm trapped here going nowhere . . . it just doesn't seem . . . ' Ruby saw the colour flow into that spot on Cook's neck and knew she'd said too much.

'Oh, you *are* going somewhere — and with my foot behind your backside, Miss Ruby May Tranton! You selfish young wench! You have no idea the loss that many on board those ships have suffered. Or their loved ones who were left behind . . . ' She breathed deeply as if fighting to control her emotions and temper. 'Get in that scullery now and start cleaning. Another word of nonsense from your mouth, and I'll show you around the docks myself; and then you can see how far a girl without work and references can go on her own!'

Ruby ran past her. There was no reasoning with the woman when her neck flushed red. Ruby screwed up her face as she entered the scullery. This was her future. With heavy heart and even heavier pans, she started her work.

★ ★ ★

Cook stayed outside in the air to try and calm down. She felt flustered; it happened more and more these days, just her time of life. However, the girl had no sense. Who called a commoner 'Ruby May', anyway? It was feeding her brain with grand notions that she was more than she could ever be, even if she should. Oh, she was pretty enough, but no one would see her to admire her, tucked away in the back of the house.

'Precisely,' she muttered and shook her head. She had lived enough years on this troubled planet to understand that asking questions did not always get the correct answers. No, she would not change her position in life. She was lucky that she had not been brought up by the banks of the Thames with a whore of a mother and the same abysmal future marked out for her.

The master had got Ruby from a good place, he said. She worked hard and was used to discipline, but her flights of fancy would dog her days if she was caught on her own — and near the marshes, too. Cook shook her head — no sense at all! Just like the master had said she'd be.

'You fine there, Mrs Grambler?' The deep voice drifted over to her.

'Very fine, young man,' Cook replied politely. Giles Marran was a good-looking young lad, like his father — the strong and once-handsome blacksmith — but he was sharp as one of her carving knives, and never missed a trick. Quick

14

of wit, that one, she thought as she greeted him with a friendly smile.

'Was that Miss Tranton that I just saw run inside?' he asked, innocently enough.

'Aye, and what if it was, lad?' she enquired as she cut a last sprig of rosemary.

'Where did he find her? Mr Sedgwick, I mean,' he added.

'Why would you want to know that, Giles Marran? And who gave you the right to call the master 'he'?'

Cook straightened up. She was a fairly stocky woman, and she eased out her spine as it cricked and creaked when she stood straight again. Middle life was not all she had hoped it would be. No man to care for her, just daily work to do and a roof over her head, so what could she expect? At least she had a sister and nieces and nephews to look out for her if she could no longer work. That was more than most. Perish the wars! Taken so many men, and left others half-men, or groping around for a decent day's work. How was a man

15

expected to be at war, killing one minute, and then to be sent home the next to act as if everything was normal again? Killing was killing and murder was murder — unless some politician told them it was fine to do it for your King, seemingly. She shook her head. Her thoughts were running off with her again: too many memories. Normally she kept busy and did not dwell on what old age would be like. She sighed as another wave of heat ran through her.

'You are sure you are well, Mrs Grambler?' he asked again, looking at her slightly bemused. 'Is something the matter?'

She held her flustered head high and stared square back at him. 'Yes, thank you! So what business is it of yours what Ruby does?' As if he could understand about things that affected women.

He smiled and shrugged his shoulders as if he cared not. 'None, really. It was just that she is quite fair and pretty, and not like . . . well, she seems different in some way to the other local girls.'

'Giles Marran, you keep your notions and high ideas away from Ruby May. If you get the gossips wagging their idle tongues about her, then her reputation will be ruined. You'll leave a young woman, with no family to turn to, in dire straits. You wouldn't want that, would you?' She waved her garden pincers at him.

'The orphanage or foundling home, then . . . ' He smiled.

'Ger off with you. You'll not find out your tittle-tattle from me.' She turned away from him to signify the end of the conversation.

'Good morning, Mrs Grambler,' he said, and winked at her as she glanced back at him over her shoulder.

Even as a mature woman, she could plainly see he was a finely built lad, with his sandy hair, almost-green eyes, and strong jawline. He had helped his father, and also gone out on his uncle's boat on the river since being a boy. He could turn his hand to all sorts, but if he turned the girl's head there would be hell to pay. No; young Ruby had a future, but not if attention was brought to her. She had to stop traipsing around like a fairy who could flit here and there on the low path without harm coming to her. This was a dangerous place; the marshes held more wildlife than just birds and fish. There was the fear of the ague. However, there was still a good trade to be had if you could land the right goods ashore. So it was mankind who could be the cause of harm to someone who was in the wrong place at the wrong time. It was Mrs Grambler's task to see that Ruby was kept at the house and kept safe. Foolish child — and even more foolish was the woman who had given birth to her.

Mrs Grambler lifted her small basket and returned to her kitchen.

'Good day, Giles Marram, now be off with you,' she shouted back as she walked away from him.

He strode off down toward the river.

Mrs Grambler looked back over her shoulder and watched him go. His walk was confident — not arrogant, like his uncle's, but Cook knew too well how easy it would be for a girl to lose her heart to such a fine-looking lad. No, she appraised him again. He was older than his youthful looks might imply. He'd gone to war as a boy, and come back as a man full-grown. His uncle had meanwhile continued his trade, using his fisherman's smack to trade contraband or anything that turned a coin. He may only own a small fishing boat, but it frequented the routes from the Barking Creek, River Roding to the Thames and the wild sea. It, like many others, bobbed along on its way catching more than cod to take to Billingsgate market, which, ironically she thought, was next to the London Customs House.

Cook knew things went on, but didn't ask any questions. But she had heard about the deep carts with false bottoms that crossed over Bow Bridge.

That girl needed to take care. Fresh out of a convent, and roaming around the marshes like she was born to them! She had heard that even people could be traded for a price — not just the slaves. She thought for a moment about her ponderings; the slaves were people too, she supposed. She shook her head to clear her mind of them, as it was too disturbing for her; she could hardly change or influence the world from the way it was.

She had become very fond of Ruby, but stiff measures would be needed if she was not to end up in a worse state than her poor mother. She shook her head. How could Master Sedgwick not realise that, with such an image of Ruby's own mother before her, she would not have seen through his lies? Perhaps the man didn't care. After all, who would she share it with? Cook had a position to keep.

Mrs Grambler stopped and took one last look across at the sails. Such a river! Magnificent, busy with trade going to all points of the globe . . . she too had once had notions. Yes, a girl could dream; but she was no girl anymore, and her charge had to see reality for herself and understand that life was no game. You couldn't just pretend and expect to survive. How to make Ruby understand so that she could see it, and understand Mrs Grambler's meaning without being scared? She had been protected by nuns, and now the master seemed to want to hide her away — as if the past was her fault.

She entered the old Hall. It was stark, isolated and unwelcoming — just as the master liked it. As she had too once . . . but those days were gone by now; it was empty, like her life had been before Ruby came home.

She swallowed and tipped her head back. 'Ruby! I can't hear nothing,' she said. Quick clangs, followed by the sounds of water splashing and someone scrubbing the pans, followed.

'That's better,' Mrs Grambler said, and smiled. Ruby was a good soul, and she had loved the last few months having her with her — but, oh, she was pretty, and before long she would realise it. Then what? Mrs Grambler picked up her cleaver and smashed it down into the feathered chicken carcass that lay lifeless on her chopping board.

3

'Did you see her, Giles?' The voice came out of the shadows of the The Bull Inn.

Giles was sitting on the settle by the fire, his tankard placed on an upturned barrel by his right knee, his lungs breathing in the heady, smoke-filled air; but his mind was wishing him far away from this area of the East End of London. Aldgate was a place he knew, but he also knew that he needed to watch his back. He would also prefer to be far away from the man who had summoned him there.

There had been no point in hiding in the shadows of the small inn, for he knew this man would seek him out, whatever place he tried to hide within.

'Go away,' Giles said quietly when the figure seated itself opposite and then took a sip of his ale. The man would not cause a scene here. Amos, the landlord, could have him out of there at the hands of the bullish-built man, Spinner, who used a solid blackthorn club with a deft skill that belied the man's dull wit. He and it together made a convincing deterrent. If only they knew who the stranger was, they'd shake in their hobnailed boots.

The man slid onto the other end of the settle. He kept his collar high, but removed his tall hat as he stared at Giles. 'That is no way to greet a friend, Giles.'

'You are no friend of mine,' he replied, still staring into the fire's low flames.

'If I am not a friend, then that would make me your enemy, Giles — and that you do not want, do you?' He glanced back to the serving hatch before adding, 'And why should you? Because neither of us wants it.' His voice was low as he smiled his words out, but Giles' chest tightened slightly despite his best efforts not to be affected by the older man's sense of menace. 'So, have you news for me of the woman I seek?'

The tallow candles flickered and filled the air with their pungent aroma. It was lost in the many odours that permeated the place, from smoke to sweat. Giles wanted to leave. He'd like to take the beauty — the jewel — that was Ruby away from this place, let her wings spread, and then see her fly into an unsuspecting world to make of it what she might. But that he could not do. This man would make sure of it. She was an innocent maid in a guilty world.

'What is she to you, anyway?' Giles asked. He stared at this stranger to the area, a man whose fine features and expensive greatcoat he loathed. No, more than that, he actually hated. He had money. His commission had been purchased with it, and his position now working for King and country had been bought by birthright, not by effort.

'Never mind that. Just remember that you owe me, and I like to collect all my debts.' He rested back.

'Are you trying to threaten me?' Giles said, wrestling with his inner demons as he spoke. For, despite everything the man stood for and represented just by being, one fact was undeniable — he had saved Giles' life, and now he owed him. But was he willing to trade the life of a young woman to pay for it, especially one as pretty as young Ruby May? Was that what would happen if the man found her? If he was seeking her out for good reasons, then why not just approach Mr Sedgwick at the Hall? He was hardly to know that the man was almost a recluse.

'Yes, of course I am. If you think for one moment you can avoid me or my command, then I remind you that you cannot.' He picked up Giles' tankard, took a long and savouring mouthful, then placed it carefully back on the barrel. 'Is that understood, Sergeant?'

'I'm not your sergeant anymore. The war is done with.' Giles glared at him. He might be indebted, but he was no longer his subordinate in rank, just in wealth.

'Perhaps not, but you answer to me. So, is the new girl the woman I seek?' he asked again, and this time leaned forward. He took a miniature out of his pocket and showed it to Giles again in case he had forgotten her likeness. Giles could see something resembling hunger in the captain's normally impassive eyes.

'I'm not sure. I only saw her fleetingly as she returned to the Hall. It was misty, and she was further away than any rifle bullet would travel.' He rubbed his hand through his hair. He wanted to be rid of his captain, of the memories, and of his debt. If his father knew that he had become a rich man's pawn, he would try and buy Giles his liberty; but this man did not want or need money, he wanted a puppet — a trained one. 'Perhaps you should call at the Hall and ask its master if you can see his maids?' he said.

The captain's eyes bore into Giles';

the mouth creased into a smile, the eyes did not. Giles fought the urge to look away. 'That would be certain folly. I will return to the forge in two weeks' time . . . '

This time it was Giles who sat forward, his fists clenched.

'Don't!' Giles snapped out the word and cursed silently at the same time. The man had him. He had shown his weakness — his father.

'Your father is a proud man . . . So happy to have his son return sound in mind and body — unscarred; a real war hero; made the rank of sergeant so young — a natural leader of men. Not one that was bought a rank of any kind, but who actually earned it. What father would not be proud to call Sergeant Giles Marran son? I could share with him memories of your inshore operations — of your ability to fire ships, and of your bravery . . . '

Giles listened with pride; yet he had protected his father from the details of the grime and gore of bloody war, and all its necessary unpleasantness. Also of the danger he had placed himself in on many occasions. 'Stop, sir; there is little glory to be had in war, as well you know.'

'Oh, I disagree. It depends how successful you are — and, of course, if you are caught . . . ' A sneer crossed his mouth.

So that was it — he would torture Giles' father with the knowledge that he had been a prisoner of Napoleon. The man did not need to know this. 'Leave him alone. Stay away . . . ' he added, but then he realised the futility of his words. 'He does not need to know details.'

'Do you remember when we saw Napoleon: such a short man wearing high boots; a restless energy raging through him? And the way his hair hung low on his forehead and down the side of his face? Did you speak with him for long on your own, Giles . . . ?'

'You know I did not!' Giles snapped.

'He was intelligent, brutal, a strategist . . . and quite, quite mad. Few of low rank have had the privilege of a direct audience. Can those who have, though, be trusted? Especially as they then return home unscathed and at liberty, no parlay or exchange, yet trouble brews with him still at large.'

'Stop it!' Giles fist rocked the barrel as it came down.

'No, I won't if I see fit to continue. Yes, I'll threaten you, Giles Marran, and anyone else, in order to find the answers to the questions I ask. So do not frustrate or annoy me in my investigation. I can save you now, as I have before; or I can put so much stain on your name that you can never be free of it again. Around these parts, they have ways of dealing with traitors and their families, so I have been told.' He sat back.

'I am no traitor, as you well know.' Giles snapped his words out as quietly as he could, for he had no wish to imply the man's accusations were correct by having their conversation overheard.

The other man tossed a coin onto the

barrel. 'My thanks to you for the drink. I'll see you here in two weeks — or, if not, we'll see how your father reacts when I tell him the things you forgot to mention about your time away.' He winked. 'In other words, I'll see you at your father's forge, where we will have a frank and open discussion about what it takes to be a 'hero'. I want you to see if it is her. Find out her name, her past, and gain her trust.' He stood up. 'Bye, Giles. Don't let me down.' He swept away through the gloom of the inn.

Giles stared at his back as it disappeared, then closed his eyes for a moment. 'Hell!' He had lived through war already, and now the peace of his home was about to be destroyed too.

He would never have betrayed his country, or his father. He had not had a private audience with the man who would rule France and beyond. Bonaparte had seen him, and on a whim had spoken to him, impressed that he had managed to single-handedly set alight a frigate, resulting in downing her. Bonaparte had apparently thought him a singularly lucky, rather than skilled, man; but changed his mind when he told him, 'But you were not so lucky because you were caught.'

Giles was only alive due to the action and quick thinking of his captain, who had known about Giles' reckless plan and turned a blind eye to it, but did not leave him to the French. His captain had done the opposite of what he had told him he would do, and had come for him.

He remembered the short conversation he had with Boney. The man was aggressive, definitely clever, but there was a restless busyness about him that had struck Giles; like a hunger that could never be sated. It was a meeting he would never own up to — because to talk about any quality in Bonaparte that could be seen as expressing admiration for him would result in Giles hanging from a gibbet, like a pirate of old, over the mud banks of the Thames.

What and who the girl was, he did

not know. He had her name — but if it was important, he had no idea why it was so. Who was she? If he was to help her, or extricate himself from the dubious demands of his ex-captain, then he had two weeks to find out the truth. He tossed the coin to the serving wench before storming out into the night.

4

Ruby woke early, as she always did. Staring out of her narrow attic window, wrapped in her blanket, she watched the distant sails. She quickly wiped her face with the cloth after dipping in the cold water from her jug that she took up with her every night. The water would be as hot as she dared to have it to carry, the steam rising as she climbed the narrow bare wooden flight of stairs off the main landing of the house. It warmed her through before she settled to bed.

She rolled up her stockings under her dress and pulled on her boots. They were still reasonably new. The master had been most generous when she arrived. Yet she had never even so much as seen, Mr Sedgwick. With her jug of cold water in her hand, she ran down the stairs and crossed the carpeted landing to enter the servants' passage down to the kitchens. These steps were made from stone, and Ruby slowed down, as they were more dangerous to fall on. She found it strange that anyone could live in a house that was like a warren of secret passages, where servants ran around unseen, usually unheard, yet always present. Perhaps in time she would learn the secrets the place held; for what else was there for her to do here, but work ceaselessly and age? Her thoughts returned to the river and the ships that constantly entered and left it, and her normally happy heart saddened as she realised she was stuck. She had longed to escape the convent and see the outside world — which she had, by coach. Who would have believed that? Yet her destination had been this desolate place. However, the river was majestic, and always different as it constantly changed.

'Morning, Ruby,' Cook said, as she entered the kitchen. A tired-looking Maisie was already scrubbing pans at the sink.

'Morning — I'm not late, am I?' Ruby asked.

'No, lass, you're not. The master is expecting guests, so we are getting a good start.' Cook glanced over at Maisie, who was stifling a yawn behind her wet hand. 'Aren't we?' she shouted over.

'Yes, Cook,' Maisie replied. 'More hands would have made lighter work, though,' she muttered.

Cook shot her a stern look, but did not say anything.

'What do you want me to do?' Ruby asked, after emptying her jug in the sink. 'Can I do the fires?' she asked hopefully.

Maisie slammed a pan down and this time Cook glared at her.

'No, Ruby, you take over from Maisie. She does the fires in the house,' Cook said, smiling back at Ruby's disappointed face.

'Then could I go with her, Mrs Grambler?' Ruby persisted. She wanted to see the rooms that surrounded this narrow maze of corridors and servitude.

For as long as she could remember, she had desperately wanted to see the world — the sinful world that she had been told so much about. Ruby did not see herself as desiring to indulge in evil wicked ways, just to understand more about what it was that she was not to covet in the first place. The journey to this strange old house had taken her across London in a closed carriage, but when they had changed horses at The Bull Inn a place called Aldgate she had seen some of the vast, dirty city, and had longed to know what else she had missed.

'You can go with Maisie and see her set the fire in the morning room, so that you know how one is done, and then you come straight back here. You hear me?' Cook waved a warning wooden spoon at her.

'Mrs Grambler!' Maisie began to protest, but Cook waved her hand to shush her and she smiled.

Maisie suddenly changed her manner. 'Very well, Cook, I'll see she comes straight back to you to do some real work,' she added, changing her tone again. She hastily dried her hands on a piece of cloth and turned to Ruby, her mouth fixed in a firm line before it reluctantly parted lips to address her. 'Come, Tranton; put on that old apron and pick up that bucket and brush, and be careful. The first thing you must learn is that fires are dirty things, and the master doesn't want you mucking up his Belgian rug!' She collected her own apron and led the way out.

Ruby eagerly followed her, but Cook tapped her on her shoulder. 'Straight back!' she reminded her.

'Of course,' Ruby replied, and smiled before following Maisie, who had already gone on ahead of her without waiting.

*　*　*

'Well, you are slow, girl. So you've much to learn,' Maisie chided her as she entered the morning room. 'Are

38

your hands clean?'

Ruby nodded; all she had done was get up, so why wouldn't they be? 'Yes,' she said.

'Good. Open the curtains and the windows a fraction to let in light and air, and then you can put this coarse cloth over the tiled hearth.' Maisie stood there as if she was Cook or the housekeeper ordering her about.

Still, Ruby had volunteered, as she was desperate to learn any new skill, and so did as she was bid. As light flooded into the room, which had once been elegant with fine cornices and a large marble fireplace surrounded by a pattern of leaves in plaster, Ruby thought that somehow it looked empty and devoid of life and love. The dust particles that glistened in the morning light caught her attention for a moment as she admired their beauty.

'Tranton!' Maisie snapped, and pointed to the rug in front of the fireplace. 'Move that away and cover the hearth with this.' The cloth she held out to her was rough and not clean at all.

'It's dirty,' Ruby noted, stating the obvious.

'Well, it would be, wouldn't it? You're a bit simple, aren't you?' Maisie snapped, and Ruby was surprised at just how much the words hurt her. 'You may have fine features and bouncy hair, becoming of a harlot, but you've not the sense you was born with.'

'That's unkind,' Ruby replied as she struggled to lift and move the rug away on her own.

'Oh dear, are you not used to such words, or heavy work? Where exactly did you come from?' Maisie asked.

'There,' Ruby said as she spread out the fabric in front of the fire, having first removed the fender.

'Now, rake out the cinders and ashes, careful like. We don't want a huge mess. So tell me, girl, where're you from?'

Ruby set to her task, being as careful as she could. It was too early in the day to fall out with someone, especially if they didn't have any real reason to dislike you. She supposed it was that the fact that Cook was so good to her, the new girl, and that had made Maisie jealous. That was not Ruby's fault, though.

'Cat got your tongue?'

'Sorry, Maisie, I was just concentrating on the task in hand.' Ruby raised the brush she was holding and smiled.

'Yep, just as I thought, you're simple. One thought, one job. You'll not get far in the Hall. Best set your sights on the laundry or dairy. Right now, though, you use this leather to wipe the grate and fire irons.' Maisie looked around her. 'My mother was once an upper housemaid here, and my father a footman. We go back a long way with the Sedgwicks. So, where did you come from?' she asked again.

Ruby was focused on what she was doing and saw no harm in sharing a little light conversation. 'I was raised in a convent,' she finally said. The less she told her, then the more curious this Maisie would become, no doubt making up stories instead. There was a silent pause, and then a wail of laughter, which stopped as Maisie remembered where they were.

'Crikey, we've got a nun working here! Oh well, that'll cheer up the lasses in the village when I tells them that you aren't after Frank, William or Giles. Good men are hard to find around these parts. Although not impossible. Sarah, who was here last year, took herself off to Barking and married a lad who had inherited his father's fishing boat. Yep, he makes his living going up and down the Roding and off to London. Mind, he was handy with his hands, if you know what I mean,' she chuckled.

Ruby was not sure that she did, but nodded and smiled up at her as if she did, as she finished her task.

'Oh, sorry,' Maisie said. 'You wouldn't, would you? Still, never mind. If you're lucky, someone will take you on. You have some looks so that will make up for the lack of wit. There's many a man prefers a woman that way,' she laughed, but when Ruby did not react to her latest insult, she seemed to give up on trying to rile her. 'Now, you take them ashes downstairs, and I'll set up the fire. You're so slow. Tomorrow, if you're allowed, you can come with me and empty the slops and the chamber pots. Then you'll really feel like part of the household.'

Maisie was obviously very good at enjoying her own poor attempts at humour, Ruby thought, but again ignored the insult. 'Thank you for letting me help with this,' Ruby said, and she saw the thick eyebrows of Maisie's dark features raise as if she were trying to figure out whether Ruby's words were meant sincerely, or if they were said in sarcasm.

Ruby smiled. The girl had dull wits, poor looks, and few opportunities in life open to her. She had no reason to add more misery to Maisie's existence by trading banter with her.

'Careful you don't trip on the stairs and get soot all over that pretty hair of yours,' Maisie said, as she knelt down to see to the fire.

Ruby left, and tiptoed down the uncarpeted servants' stairs to the kitchen. She saw Cook, who looked relieved that she had returned.

'Ah, good, lass; now take the bucket out to the far corner of the walled garden and empty it. The gardener likes his ash.' Cook winked at her; Ruby was not sure why, but she smiled back anyway.

'What for?' Ruby asked.

'How should I know? Get about your business and stop asking questions, and then return to me. You can have your breakfast and then get on with the preparation. Go . . . ' She waved her hands, hurrying Ruby out of the door.

'Yes, Mrs. Grambler,' she said, and shivered as she stepped out into the cold morning air.

Ruby walked briskly through the mist of the early morning. She jumped sideways as a figure emerged through the east gate of the walled garden. Thinking it must be Barnabas the gardener, up and about his business, she gave the figure a welcoming smile. He was an old man and rarely woke early, so she was happy that he must be feeling well this morning.

It was plain to see as the man neared that this figure stood tall and proud, with no hint of age wearing those muscular shoulders down. He did not bend or stoop like tired old Barnabas. He seemed to be staring at her feet, which puzzled Ruby.

She glanced down, though; soot had flopped over the edge of the bucket and onto her skirt. 'No!' Ruby's head shot up, accusing eyes glaring back at the figure — a man she thought had no business being there.

'Ruby?' Giles asked. 'It is Ruby, isn't it?' His voice was welcoming and inquisitive, but she was annoyed by his presence, her situation, and what he would think of such a clumsy dotehead.

'Look what you made me do! Mrs Grambler will be furious! And I'm to prepare food later.' She plonked the bucket down with such force that it spilled some more of the contents over her boots. Her eyes moistened, but she was not going to whimper like a child in front of Giles Marran.

Without speaking, he took the bucket and emptied the contents in the pile at the corner of the garden; then quickly returned to Ruby, who stood transfixed like a statue, blankly staring down at the damage. She did not know what to do.

'Here, come with me.' He held out a hand to her.

Hers lifted to touch his, but as soon as she did, the warmth of his rough fingers made her pull back. What was she thinking of? If she was seen holding his hand, it would look . . . well, bad. She could be dismissed on the spot.

'Ruby, I can help you,' he added, and dropped his hand to his side, gesturing instead that they should head towards the stable block.

Apprehensively, she followed. She sniffed back tears; he looked back at her, but she merely shrugged. ''Tis the cold,' she explained.

He smiled. Ruby knew that the other girls like Maisie had a soft spot for Giles Marram. He had returned something of a hero; and, being so hale, hearty and free, had turned the heads of the local women. His father had a good trade, too. Whoever married Giles would not need to toil for long days from five in the morning till whenever they were dismissed.

She watched him disappear inside and reappear with handfuls of fresh dry hay. He bent low at her feet, and started to flick the soot from her skirts and then her boots. The dry powder fell away until all that was left was a slightly darker tint to the weave of the cloth. 'There: when you can, you can rinse that bit off and dry it in front of the kitchen range. Cook will understand, she's not an ogre. You be fair with her, and she'll be good to you,' he said as he stared up at her.

'Thank you.' She watched as he stood straight up without stepping

47

back, so that his tall frame was only inches in front of her. She could feel the warmth from his body. His head passed hers as he straightened until she was staring at the stubble of his chin.

'You are most welcome.' He smiled at her as his words, spoken so politely, dripped off his honeyed tongue. Then he glanced back toward the house. 'Can I walk you back?'

'No, I shouldn't be taking so long to do this simple chore. Cook will wonder what I've been doing . . . ' She blushed, realising that her words could imply that she knew she *could* have been doing something with him, which was not what she meant at all. ' . . . and if you were seen here, with me . . . ' Her last comment had not helped her awkwardness.

'It would be very embarrassing and dangerous to your reputation if I told them that I had flicked your skirts and glimpsed your slender ankle.' He winked, and she could not help but chuckle, despite her determination to remain aloof.

'I am wearing boots, Mr Marram,'

she said quietly.

'You are Miss Ruby May Tranton, are you not?' he said, his eyes quite focused on hers, his expression more serious.

'Why do you ask?' Ruby picked up the bucket and began walking back.

'I have heard of your beauty, and I . . . ' he began; but she glanced back at him, laughed, and ran back to the kitchens.

Strange man, she thought. If he could pour such sweet words out of his mouth, so smooth and so early in the day, then he was one to watch . . . and possibly stay away from.

★ ★ ★

Giles watched her go. It was cold, but she was like a breath of warm fresh air to him. She had something about her manner that made his heart smile. Oh! He groaned at that thought. He was thinking like a lovelorn puppy, not a man who had seen war. That made him turn on his heel and walk back towards the marshes where he would meet with his Uncle Josiah. Another man filled his mind, though — his ex-captain, Edwin Adolphus Miles, who he owed his life and reputation to. But why did he want to find Ruby May? Miles had a miniature of a woman who looked amazingly like the girl, and that made him wonder who that woman was. The miniature was exquisitely made, which suggested that whosoever the woman in the image was, she was from a moneyed family. Did he seek a likeness of her? If so, did that put the innocent young Ruby in danger?

He had two weeks to find out all that he could, and then he would decide how he could escape from being both the man's puppet and possibly Ruby May's downfall. He could not charm her so easily; this woman was going to need a very different approach to the ever-flirtatious Maisie Dowson. He could have that girl's company any time he chose, if he were blind and foolish enough to.

5

It was eight hours later before Ruby finally managed to leave the Hall again. She had been warming the bedchamber ready for the elusive Mr Sedgwick, whom she had yet to set eyes upon, to retire. She carried the cleaning bucket and jug of dirty water down with her to the kitchens. Twice in one day she had been allowed above stairs. Maisie had been tired, and Cook had taken her break early, so Ruby had jumped at the chance.

Emptying the water into the stone sink, she was surprised to see Maisie's figure still slumped and half-asleep in Mrs Grambler's favourite chair. Her legs were precariously balanced on a three-legged stool that looked as if it had been there since Wat Tyler led the peasants' revolt.

'Maisie, why are you sitting there?' Ruby asked.

Maisie jumped, her feet shot off the stool, and she sat bolt upright. Her cloth cap rested at an angle as her dark unkempt hair tried to break free. She looked as if her body had responded before her wits, and it was all Ruby could do not to laugh out loud. This girl had taunted Ruby mercilessly. She always wanted to mark her position out as senior, now she had someone below her in rank to pick on. Yet right now she looked like a dishevelled serving wench. Ruby bit back her instincts to retaliate, and realised she did not really know what a dishevelled serving wench in an inn looked like, but guessed that it was something resembling the annoyed stirring mess in front of her. Before the woman could vent her anger at Ruby again, she gave her a question to think on quickly. 'Didn't Mrs Grambler tell you to take the order down to Mrs Sessions?'

Maisie's face paled. She had had a busy day and was not the most agile of young women. 'Damnation! I forgot all about it.' She groaned and stood up reluctantly.

'I'll go,' Ruby said, grasping her chance. 'You showed me the fires this morning,' she added, 'so I can do this for you now.'

'Aye, I did, and you threw me whole day into chaos as a result of holding me up. You go instead, and be quick back, or you'll get us both into trouble. Mrs Grambler's snoring away on her nap, so waste no more time.' She plonked herself back down in her chair. 'And remember, old Sessions is a right gossip, so don't go talking to her about the Hall and things that don't concern her. If she needs to know aught, she can see me on Friday when she delivers!'

'No, Maisie, I won't,' Ruby replied sweetly, and could not believe her good fortune. She had an errand to run that Maisie had forgotten all about, and needed young legs to deliver Mrs Grambler's note. So with glee she wrapped her woollen shawl around her shoulders and headed off to the village.

The cottage she sought was on the outskirts, but that was close enough for her to feel that she had explored the area further. It needed to be because of the noxious hum from the animals Mrs Sessions kept. Even with the courtyard between the pigs and the cottage, when the wind travelled in the wrong direction Ruby could smell it at the door. Maisie had said how it would do her good, as it was supposed to help a bad chest — but Ruby did not have one anyway. Cook was always warning Ruby of going near the marshes lest she catch the ague. She had not been brought up in these parts, and that was supposed to make her some kind of weakling, one who would fall sickly at the slightest chill. But what Cook did not realise was that the convent was cold, with damp air common, and also had been near the flat fenland. As a child, Ruby had cheated death after months of fevers and bed rest. The weakness had taken a year to overcome, but overcome it she had. Her delicate appearance belied a will as strong as iron and a faith to match.

Ruby knew she was one of life's survivors. She smiled to herself; she seemed much stronger and healthier than most of the few people she had seen. Perhaps the exception was Giles Marram . . . She shook her head. Why should he pop into her mind again?

Running down the lane, she saw Marsh Cottage, almost hidden behind a wild blackthorn that had been left to grow wild. The cottage was quite overgrown with ivy, looking as though it would be reclaimed by nature at any moment.

Ruby pushed open the gate that squeaked so loud it could have warned half of the village that a stranger was approaching. She wondered why it had not been oiled, but then perhaps her initial thought answered that question for her.

She raised her hand to knock on the old wooden door — as there was no sign of a knocker to lift — when it opened. The sound of a large bolt being drawn made her take a step back before the door moved.

'Yes?' An old woman greeted her. Thin and willowy in looks, her stare was powerfully strong as it bore into Ruby. Her eyes were like the grey mist that hung over the Thames some days.

'I have a note . . . an order for you from Mrs Grambler,' Ruby explained, holding out the message.

'Thank thee,' she said, and slipped it into her skirt pocket without glancing at it first. 'Would you come in out of the chill?' she asked.

The cottage may have looked less than welcoming or homely, but the woman who owned it seemed friendly enough. However, remembering Maisie's warning and aware that her time was running away with her again, Ruby hesitated.

'I really have to get back, but thank you — perhaps another time.' Ruby stepped back, but the woman's hand shot out and took hers.

'Just for a moment, it is quite lonely

here. I'm not used to seeing such a pretty face on me own doorstep.' She smiled an uneven grin, showing gaps and teeth that seemed too thin for the mouth that housed them.

'I'm sorry . . . ' It was all Ruby could do to get away without being dragged inside. Mrs Sessions had hens and pigs that she sold to the Hall as and when needed. In return, Cook often kept a loaf back for her when she baked Mr Sedgwick's bread.

'Ah, now, aren't you a fine sight for sorry eyes,' Mrs Sessions blurted out as she held on and gave her arm a gentle tug. 'What does she ask for this time?' she asked and looked directly at Ruby.

'I've no notion, Mrs Sessions, as I've not read it. I was just asked to deliver it quickly and return straight back.' Ruby looked at the woman's hand as if to offer a polite plea that she might relinquish her grip.

'Oh, surely you can come in and have a chat,' she persisted. 'You being new up at the Hall, you won't know much

57

about the local people. We don't get many foreigners in these parts,' she added.

'I'm not foreign,' Ruby explained, rather puzzled at the notion. Sister Marianne had been French; she was one of the younger nuns in the convent. She had escaped when her family had been targeted in the revolution. Now, *that* was foreign, but it was also quite exotic in Ruby's eyes.

'No, maybe not in a worldly sense — but you're not from these parts, that's all I mean. So, where *are* you from?' she asked. 'You from town?'

'No, I was . . . '

'Ruby!' The male voice nearly made her jump as it was so unexpected. She saw Mrs Sessions' genial expression harden.

'Pardon?' Ruby turned around to see Giles Marran standing in the lane.

'Mrs Grambler sent me to see you back safely to the Hall. Don't want you getting lost, now, do we?' He opened the small gate; the shriek of metal scraping against raw metal made Ruby cringe. Giles stood waiting for her to go to him.

'None of your business, son,' Mrs Sessions said, releasing Ruby, and folding her arms under her bosom. 'The lass has a mind of her own.' The ugly grin leered at Ruby as she continued, 'Don't you, girl?' The gappy smile made Ruby want to run straight into Giles' strong, protective arms.

Ruby stood firm and tried to smile genuinely back. 'I don't want to upset Mrs Grambler, though, she can get quite flustered.'

' 'Tis only her flux,' Mrs Sessions said, but Giles quickly interrupted when he saw Ruby's puzzled expression.

'It is my business if Cook wants her back and I gave my word to fetch her safely.' He stared back at the woman — a silent challenge, almost palpable, hung in the cool air between them.

'Aye, if she did!' the woman muttered under her breath. She glanced from one to the other. Ruby felt as if there was an unspoken dialogue going on between these two people. It made her feel uneasy, but she was more inclined to trust Giles Marram than this strange imposing woman. Why, she was unsure. However, she did what she normally did and followed her instinct. It had rarely let her down.

'Coming, Mr Marram.' She nodded politely to Mrs Sessions and slipped out of the gate and into the lane. She made sure that as she walked back up to the Hall there was at least a good foot between her and Giles. The last thing she wanted was for the local gossips to decide that she was the war hero's latest conquest.

'You could not have been sent by Cook,' Ruby said after a few awkward silent moments.

'I know that and you know that, but that nosy old witch doesn't,' he replied.

'That is quite harsh. She is an old woman, not a witch,' Ruby protested. 'People can be quite ignorant where superstition is concerned. Giles, you should take care what you say about whom.'

'Ruby, you are very naïve about this area and the folk thereabouts. She may not mix potions and recite incantations of the devil, but that tongue of hers would sell her own soul if it meant she could catch hold of the latest gossip and turn profit as a result of it. Information is money. Please do not be fooled by a crooked smile and a few kind words.' He had stopped and turned so that he stood before her.

'Yours or hers?' she replied, and saw a glint of humour in his eyes.

'I think you know fine well who I meant.' He seemed to relax as he watched her.

'What are you? A man who stalks his prey? A nosey parker? A guardian angel?' She looked up into pale blue eyes that seemed to be so openly smiling back at hers. 'Or someone who seeks to make profit?'

'I would like to think the latter. I am curious about this new maid, who is rarely seen out unless she ventures onto the marsh — also not recommended. Who are you, Miss Tranton? From where did you appear?' he asked. His head tilted slightly as if he was studying a puzzle.

'Miss Ruby May Tranton — ' She dipped a curtsey as she spoke. ' — at your service — or at least at the Hall's service.'

'I know your name, but where did they pick you from, and who was your father? What did your father do?' he asked.

'I have no idea,' came her surprisingly bold reply. She slipped around him and began walking back to the Hall.

'I don't understand.' He strode alongside her, not letting the matter drop.

'I grew up in a convent. I was left there, and my parents did not tell their details to the nuns. So, you see: I may be an orphan; I may be from a poor family who could not feed me; or I could be purely the unwanted child of a loveless match — perhaps even an illegitimate one, the result of the sin of a fallen woman.' She spoke with confidence that she did not feel, but would not shirk from the truth or possibilities she had considered over the years of her waking life, the questions that had dogged her dreams — who had given her life on earth. She did not imagine that she had been created by divine intervention.

'I'm sorry. I did not mean to cause you hurt or embarrassment.' He softened his voice.

'You did not cause either, for I was cared for, educated, and loved by my friends,' she explained, and then shrugged. 'I am what I am, just as you are the war hero, the son of the blacksmith, and the local . . . ' She flushed and carried on walking.

'The local . . . ?' he said and cupped her elbow so that she had to face him.

'The local . . . 'charmer', or so I've been warned . . . told!' She yanked her elbow free.

He laughed. 'Is that why you always

run from me?' he asked, his face creased with open glee at the thought.

'I do not!' she replied, but felt childish as it came out somewhat petulantly.

'Do so . . . ' he said softly.

'Very well. I have heard that you break hearts, and I do not intend to let anyone do that to me.' She walked on again. 'Thank you for rescuing my skirt earlier, and my time just now.'

He did not instantly follow. She glanced back, wondering if she had deeply offended Giles. She had no real reason to hold a grudge against him.

He stepped out and caught up with her again.

'I can see why some may take that view, but I do not break hearts, Ruby; nor have I sought to find myself a wife or walk out with anyone here, by choice. I have needed time to recover from being at war. Do not believe it is noble or right — death never is. I've enjoyed seeing my father again, and knowing he is still strong and able. So, you see, you have been warned off someone who wishes you no harm.'

'I have never thought it so.' Ruby felt sorry for him because his words were filled with raw emotion. She did not see a man who was a flatterer of women, but a deeply sensitive soul who was coming to terms with experiences forced upon him in a most brutal way. 'Very well, but I must go. Dinner will be finished.' She walked on, but Giles stayed and just watched her leave.

6

Giles returned down the lane, cutting through the hedgerow and passing behind the old and dilapidated Marsh Cottage. Its roof was in desperate need for a re-thatch. The air, the damp and the many years that had passed by since it was first built had all taken their toll upon it. The early evening light was fading fast.

He ducked behind the overgrown hedgerow and stood silently watching. There, out of sight, he waited; following his instincts, but not understanding or questioning why. After years creeping behind enemy lines as a skirmisher, he had learnt to listen to his 'spirit' — the inner voice that had led him out of many a dangerous situation. It was not something he could explain. Although he was not deeply religious, Giles believed strongly in good and evil, and in a guiding light that had steered him away from trouble on many an occasion. Whenever the old woman was about, his hackles rose and his senses sharpened. She had the look of cold-heartedness that he had seen so many times in the eyes of an enemy amidst the fury of a battlefield. Hers was a quiet, simmering menace, though. The fragile old woman she had acted in front of Ruby did not wash with him.

So, Giles watched her cottage for a few moments, and was shortly rewarded for his vigilance when a door opened and he saw Flora Sessions leave via the back of her home. Wrapped in an old shawl held tightly around her shoulders, and with a floppy hat upon her head, she stepped hurriedly out into the night. She did not go far, though, before disappearing into the broken-down outbuilding which was behind the pigsty.

If she had been a witch, it would not have surprised him, for she certainly had many of the attributes associated with them. He shivered involuntarily at the thought. An open enemy, one could defeat — but if she dealt with potions and hexes, then she dabbled in a realm that he did not want to enter. Her hands were twisted and her hair knotted. The besom behind the back door looked unused, and he smiled as he wondered if she used it when she did her incantations. Then another shiver ran down his spine as he realised it was possible she was a vessel or channel for evil. He blinked away such superstitious nonsense; no doubt it came from sharing too many stories with the old men of the village and his father around the open fire in the inn.

He did not ponder the notion further, for a few minutes later Flora Sessions pushed her way out of the shed door and bustled back to the cottage. She placed her hand flat on the old door, paused, and then glanced over her shoulder, her face falling into the darkness, before she completed her journey by ducking inside the outhouse.

He was about to turn away when he saw a flicker of light from inside the room, followed shortly by the old cloth, which hung as a curtain across it, being moved — twice slowly, and then twice in quick succession. Next, he realised a lamp was being lit and placed carefully on the windowsill. It was a low burning flame, but on a night such as this it was strong enough to be seen beyond the across open fields or marshes.

Giles folded his arms across his body, the air was cooling, but as he hunkered down, cradled by the bushes, he prepared to sit it out and wait to see what occurred next — or, perhaps more to the point, *who*. If she were using this simplest of methods to signal someone, then that person would soon make their move.

Then another thought crossed his mind: could he possibly slip into the outbuilding and retrieve whatever it was she had left there? Smiling to himself at the thought of a mystery afoot, Giles moved stealthily in the shadows as he had so many times in a foreign land miles away from home. He felt that strange rush of emotions stir that he had not experienced since he left his regiment. Though here he knew the ground and the climate so well, after being away for such a time, the people around him felt so different. It was actually, he realised, him that had changed. He was surprised that the familiarity of sensations and rush of feelings that filled his being pleased him. Giles felt alive again, not hiding in this place called home where he was constantly restless. Strange: he had thought he hated the war with a vengeance, but now he could see like a bolt of lightning that there were parts of him that had revelled in the drama of the moment, such as crossing over the invisible borders to spy inside enemy lines and collect information.

He pulled at some dry twigs, breaking them free of the woody briar of the blackthorn bush before quickly scattering a few behind him as he approached the old door. Once he had slipped behind the door that barely still hung on a makeshift leather hinge, he put his back to the wall and closed his eyes tightly for a moment. The total black instantly before him would help him to see through the inner murk of the outhouse as he opened them again.

Giles could vaguely see the outlines of tack and tools that were nailed on one wall; a couple of barrels were stacked in the corner with what looked like grain sacks piled behind and around them. To his immediate right was the upturned ruin of a broken gig. It had long since ceased usage and provided the only possibility of cover.

He stepped into the centre of the building and gently pushed over an upturned clay pot. Crouching to set it right, he realised that a note had been flicked out from under it. So was this what the old witch was hiding? There was not enough light in there to be able to make out more than just the form of the folded paper. Giles picked it up, but then heard the unmistakable sound of feet deftly making their way across broken twigs. He tossed the note back in its hiding place and slipped under the gig, coiling himself into its upturned form.

He slowed his breathing and waited, as surely enough the door was flung open and the sound of hurried footsteps entered as the message, whatever it was, was retrieved.

Giles used his strength to press the carriage sides and prevent himself from dropping to the ground. He tried to turn slightly to glimpse through a crack in the broken carriage, but he could not see who had taken the note. As soon as he heard the door pushed back to its original position, he lightly dropped down to the floor and crouched lest someone else be there. When the door began to open again, he was like a cat that pounced back to safety. He could tell by the uneven gait and the shuffling of skirts that it was the old widow Sessions returning. She sniffed as she breathed, and often coughed — from habit or ill health, nobody knew or cared. Sessions was a lonely soul. There was no way that woman could creep up on anyone — whether it was dark or not.

Then she lifted the pot and scooped up something that jingled, like a small coin purse, from underneath.

Giles had wanted to follow whoever it was that had retrieved the note, but now they would be long gone.

Sessions shuffled to the door; turned her head back, looking around the small space inside; and sniffed, as if the air was betraying his presence. She did not linger, though, and was soon gone.

Quietly, he dropped back to the earth and peered through a crack in the wood to see Sessions making her way back to her lair. Rather than risk being seen, he waited for the moment that she stepped inside her cottage before running for the hedgerow to make his way back down to the forge.

Was it a coincidence that Ruby had delivered a note from the Hall that same evening? Had she unwittingly played a part in the shenanigans of a trade she knew nothing of? Or was it a totally different kind of note? He doubted the witch could write. He shook his head; it was a mystery to solve. However, he wanted to leave this place, and his spirits lifted as he returned home.

It was with a happier and more peaceful heart that he saw his father still working, crafting some ornate piece of metal to adorn a gateway in one of the finer homes toward the river towns of Grays or Purfleet further along the Thames.

'Aha, my wandering son returns! You been taking a tumble with that Maisie from the old Hall?' he asked, and raised his eyebrow as he glanced at his son.

Giles shrugged it off. It was none of his father's business where he found his pleasure, but as he did not find that kind of pleasure near his home, it was a redundant question.

'Lad, believe me, being on your own is no good for a handsome young buck like you. She may not be pretty, or fresh as a maid should be, but she's willing and has a fine pair of . . . '

'Father!' Giles snapped back.

His father laughed. 'Oh, you'd turn away a warm, willing wench who can cook and no doubt give you a healthy brood?'

'You know I set my sights higher than that,' Giles said defensively whilst removing the fragment of briar from his shirt. It was cold, he was cold; and although he did not want to be talked to like a boy still wet behind the ears, it was still good to be near the flame in the forge and feel warm again.

'Aye, you've standards now, have you? But, lad, you're no longer in uniform, you're one of the returners; and, lucky as that is, many aren't fortunate enough to have a father of good trade, for many have little or none — either father or trade. If you want to catch a wench, do so before all the other soldiers return and turn their heads with tales of great bravery.' He shrugged. 'Listen, lad, it's good advice. Don't look at me like I'm an old fool.' There was no response. 'So where have you been then?' his father persisted, whilst he hammered the tempered steel into place.

'Walking, just taking the air; visiting places I grew up in and played around in before the world went mad and I had to stop playing and start killing.' He paused as his father looked over anxiously at his son. But Giles instantly regretted his comment and continued, 'It helps me to clear my head.' He seized the pincers that kept the metal in place. The blacksmith happily relinquished his grip on them so that the pair could work together in harmony, Giles holding and his father hammering.

'Still have dreams, then — or should I say nightmares?' his father asked him.

'Not really . . . well, sometimes,' he admitted. To deny he had been affected would only be a hollow boast — who would not be affected by war? He had grown from a naïve boy to a man who had killed men, earning promotion quickly through his quick wit and daring. Giles thought to change the subject. 'Tell me, Father, what do you know of the old witch . . . you know, the widow Sessions? I don't remember her before I left.'

'Well let's see . . . She is old, and she is a widow. But I'd be right careful who you label a witch, lad. Any help?'

'Just wondered what she does, that's all.' Giles tried to look casually away. He did not want to admit that he had been prying where he had no business.

His father stopped hammering momentarily and looked at him. 'I know one thing, Giles: she minds her own business and expects others to do the same. She's an old woman, so leave her be.'

Giles shrugged. 'So what about Mr Sedgwick? Have you seen him about recently?' Asking the question made him realise that this was a strange place he returned to. There was a new master of the Hall, yet he had not seen hide or hair of him in three months. A new servant has been brought back from one of Mrs Grambler's rarer trips away from the place, and this had led to the surprising visit from his old captain asking and snooping about her. The old woman had not been in the Marsh cottage before he left, as it had been in the Fairman family for generations — yet she had somehow taken up residence in the place, and made it, and herself, look like she belonged there.

'You are a curious sort now, are you not, my son? This is your home. Return, enjoy, and stop asking so many questions. Aye, Sedgwick, he was here, or his footman was with the carriage — run-down thing it is now — must have been only a couple of weeks ago. Fixed the shaft strap for him, I did,' he explained before thumping his hammer down again. Giles winced so as not to catch a flash spark in the eye.

'But did you actually see him?' Giles persisted.

'Well, not then, but later the day it was collected and he went by in it. Saw him then right enough.' His father released the pincers, after taking them back from Giles.

'What does he look like?' Giles asked.

'High hat, fine coat, he had his arm rested on the open window.'

'Grey hair, dark hair, big nose, hook nose, beard?' Giles persisted to stress his point.

'Very well. I didn't get a good look at his face, but who else would it be?'

'Exactly my point, Father — who else could it be?'

His father shook his head. 'You best go get yourself something to eat. I'll finish up here. But, Giles, you know what curiosity did to the cat . . . '

Giles nodded and walked past his father, who was admiring his handiwork, but then the man stopped him with his free hand.

'Giles, take my advice — be careful where you walk, and what questions you ask, and of whom. You are my son, but you have been away for over four years. Things change, people change, times change.' He looked at Giles, but then his vision settled somewhere beyond him.

'How have they changed, Father?' he asked quietly. 'Tell me so I may be wiser . . . '

Someone was approaching. His father nodded to them.

Giles glanced over his shoulder. 'Evening, Uncle Josiah,' he said in greeting. 'What brings you here so late?'

'Ah! Giles still asking questions — you were always such an inquisitive child.' He slapped Giles on his back. 'Still, now you're back you'll be able to keep your pa company and even give him a hand. We are none of us getting any younger, eh!'

'Let him be, he needs to find his feet again.'

'Asking questions is how you find things out, Uncle.' Giles winked at his father, who was giving him a knowing — or possibly warning — look in return.

'I just wanted to see my dear brother and his kin. Also left it a bit late, so how about somewhere to kip for the night?' His uncle smiled, revealing one solitary gold tooth amidst a mouth of brown tainted ones.

'You're always welcome, Josiah, you know that.' Giles' father gestured that he should take his uncle into the house behind the forge.

'Come, Uncle; I'll find you some ale, and you can rest up and tell me about your hard day.' He slapped his uncle on the shoulder, man to man, to show that he was no longer a boy.

7

Ruby wanted to see the sun's light fade over the river. She could go down the servants' stairs, across the kitchens and out into the yard, but then she might be spotted by Mrs Grambler. If she went through the front of the house, though, she could sit by the window in the library and watch, fascinated, till the sun had disappeared. Then the master would have finished eating and she could clear his dinner plate away.

Throwing care aside, she chose the latter. It was a room filled with knowledge that had been little used or shared. It was as if it was caught in time, but still a low fire was lit each evening and the room was frequently dusted and cleaned. Why? The phantom that was Mr Sedgwick had never been there on any of her previous visits — which, as her confidence grew, had become more frequent.

Her favourite books were about the world. She should not touch them, but the nuns had taught her how to read, and she was keen to know as much as she could. One peek inside *Candide* by a man called Voltaire had led a wide-eyed Ruby to read a few more pages. It was not a book that the sisters would have approved of in the convent, as it was worldly — and, despite it spreading a message of 'all being for the best', the world described was far from 'best' or 'Godly'.

Ruby took the novel from its position at the end of the shelf above the chair by the fire and sat down on the window cushion. There was still a little time before darkness fell. So she opened the pages, and by the failing light read just one more page.

'I trust you are not inconvenienced by the lack of a taper being lit?' a smooth male voice stated out of the silence.

Ruby stood up and carelessly dropped the novel from her fingers. Panicking, she quickly scooped it up before she could answer or look to see who addressed her. The voice had come from the shadows at the other end of the room. Once she had smoothed the volume's pages and closed it, she quickly ran to the shelf to replace the novel before he could inspect it for possible damage.

'Sorry!' She snapped the words out and quickly ran to the door, but her hand was grasped firmly as she tried to turn the handle.

'Not so quickly,' he said. She was pulled around to face the tall figure, an outline in the dusk — her hand still held.

'I meant no harm . . . ' she said. Her eyes adjusting, she realised this figure was wearing a greatcoat and tall hat. If it were the master, then why would he be dressed so, when he should be having dinner in the dining room? 'You are not Mr Sedgwick. Who are you?'

'I have been remiss, Miss Tranton, in not introducing myself beforehand. Please, come back and sit with me by the window. It is your preferred place of rest — or hiding place away from your duties — is it not?'

He led her away from the door, not taking her protest or her defiance into account. 'Let go of me, sir, or I shall . . . '

He stopped. She could feel his stare.

'What will you do?' he asked gently. 'If you scream, you betray yourself, for you are here where no servant should be, and reading the books no young lady — respectable young lady, that is — should. You are a servant who has both nerve and education.' He paused and looked at the replaced *Candide*. 'My, you have revolutionary tastes, do you not?'

'I do not . . . I do not know what you mean, sir. Who are you?' Ruby tried to wrestle her hand away from his, but he merely brushed her effort aside as he sat her down again on the window seat. She looked up at him: under the broad brim was the face of a man in his thirties. He seemed smooth-shaven and looked to be of good health and wealth. 'Who are you, and how do you know my name?' A feeling of foreboding swelled within her as she realised he had called her 'Miss Tranton'. He knew her name, and that she could be found there. Yet he acted like an imposter within the Hall's walls. But he was also correct that if she screamed, she would then have to explain why she was in the library to begin with.

'Where is your father?' he asked.

Ruby was taken aback. How was she to know that, when she had no idea who he was? She decided to answer honestly. 'I have no idea. Now I must go to the kitchen. Mrs Grambler will be wondering where I have got to.' She stood up. He pushed her back down.

She gasped, but he placed a gloved finger to her lips.

'She should be more careful where she leaves her maids, then. So, when was the last time you saw him?' he persisted.

'Who?' Ruby asked, whilst glancing

at the door and wondering if she dared to kick the man hard, somewhere . . . delicate. Could she make a break for it and get to Cook before anyone raised the alarm?

'Your father! Don't even think of it, Miss Tranton, I'd have you pinned and down before you took one stride from me. I am not a naïve wench like you, even if you choose to read . . . and read such lascivious tracts as Voltaire's drivel; you are only playing with the folly of the mind. So look to your physical safety, even if your moral one is indeed in great peril.'

Ruby thought he talked like one of the sisters when having a rant about the ways of the world, but she was hardly in a position to debate theology with him. Her mind was not in any moral danger. She sought knowledge, not to follow a foreign man's view of the world.

'I merely wanted to read a novel. I did not know which one it was, I just picked it out at random.' Her defiant words lacked conviction.

'You had no business reading anything. You are a woman. Your mind is meant, as is your body, for other pastimes. Leave politics and wisdom to your menfolk. Talking of which, your father was here *when*?' He crouched down lower so that he rested on his haunches. His eyes seemed dark in the half-light. She had placed a hand behind her back, and slowly it had found the catch of the window. *Perhaps*, she thought — but kept her eyes cast down, for this man who was ignorant in his opinions was not so when reading the mind of a trapped or cornered woman.

'My father? I do not know what you mean. I am merely a kitchen maid. My father would not be here, even if he knew . . . or I knew . . . You seek someone else . . . ' She looked out of the window, turning her head away, sad to realise that she had missed the moment in time she had come to witness, as darkness was now quickly descending.

He laughed. It was stilted and silenced, but Ruby's reply had surprised him.

'Oh, Miss Tranton, you're a treasure. You have no idea at all how precious and how vulnerable you are. Very well. I shall leave the maid to return to her work, and shall see you again — perhaps when the time is more fitting. For now, forget me. Our meeting will be our little secret. You can hardly explain where you were, and I . . . well, I shall enter by the main door next time . . . maybe.' He stood up smoothly, as if he was literally growing out of his crouched position, with no effort at all.

'Who are you?' Ruby asked, staring at him; he had the smell of the salt marshes about him that she knew so well. He had arrived from the river. 'Why do you know my name and my father?' She was standing now, her fists balled at her sides, her eyes fixed on this phantom who stepped back into the shadows. The last she saw of him was a doffed hat as he seemed to blend into the wall behind.

Ruby felt a momentary waft of cold air enter the room. She ran to the corner where he should be, but all that was there was a panel of books. It must be a false door. Quickly, Ruby tilted the novels she could reach, but to no avail. She tried to push one side and then the other. But there was no give. The man knew this house and its secrets well — but how? Ruby was angered more than frightened, because she needed to know how she was involved.

She stifled a sob of frustration. If only she knew who her father was. What he was! Then she would know what to do. Then a thought struck her like an axe cleaving a fallen tree — he lived! The man who had given her life still was very much alive. He must be important in some way. She was not an orphan, perhaps she was illegitimate — she had a father, and people expected him to find her.

From the brink of confused despair, she breathed deeply. *I am wanted!* She thought the words over slowly, repeating them in her mind: *I am truly wanted, and somehow my father is in trouble. He has people seeking him out — not nice people.*

She stared back out of the window at the evening and the reflection of the moon's strong glow. These people were from the shadows, and Ruby May Tranton now knew she had a mission in life. She would seek out her true father and help him. For she was sure it could only be a good person who had placed her in a convent where she would be brought up with an education and respect for God. So, she reasoned, if she was the lure, she now had to turn her father's arrival from one of perilous ambush to one of escape and freedom for them both.

Ruby stormed out of the room and down to the kitchens. She had to think; so, while she set about the most tedious of tasks, seeing to the pots, she would think deeply — and pray, for she needed help.

8

Giles entered the smithy and ducked his head into the barrel of water that stood outside the back of the forge. He flicked his sodden locks back as he stood up, and used his fingers to wring out the excess water. His head, now cooled, was no more settled than it had been when he had risen early in the morning and walked along through the morning mist.

In the last week since his uncle's unexpected visit, not a lot had happened. He had not managed to approach Ruby May again, only see her occasionally at a distance. It was as if Mrs Grambler was keeping her indoors on purpose. The woman was behaving like a strict governess — but Ruby was neither gentry nor a child, and certainly Grambler was in no way qualified. Yet if Ruby was in the garden picking herbs,

Grambler stood nearby looking on. She had seen him watching, and straight away sent her charge indoors. So what had changed?

Ruby no longer ambled down by the fort. Perhaps she had taken notice of his warning. Yet the way her lovely face had looked around for . . . him, searching the reason for her sudden withdrawal back to the kitchen, he suspected there was more to it. He had to see her and find out what was going on.

The carriage had been out once in the week with windows half-covered by curtains. So who was wearing the top hat?

The old woman had been quite cool with him when he entered the walled garden, as if she was deflecting all normal chatter. He definitely understood his presence was not wanted.

He leaned on the doorway to the back of the forge, and watched his father labouring away. He half-smiled, for the man was proud of every task he undertook. When his father spoke, it was, as always, with surety that his son was behind him. The man seemed to sense whenever he was being watched. Perhaps it was that second sense that had enabled Giles to survive behind enemy lines.

'What is wrong with you, Giles?' His father's hammer hit the metal on the anvil with force that made sparks fly. There was an edge to his voice that made his question sound troubled.

Giles wondered where and how to begin. He had found out so little about Ruby. He wanted to be near to her in many ways, but he had one more week before trouble would arrive, when his former Captain returned and dogged his door once more. Giles decided to start by probing about the person nearest to his family and home who concerned him the most.

'Uncle Josiah,' he said.

'If you are going to blow hot and cold, you may as well use those bellows.' His father glanced at him. 'Nigh on a week has gone by since he stayed, and still you brood. He only asked you to consider helping him out on his night trips. You're a natural, you're trained, and you are family, son.'

'Yes, Father, and do you defend a man who is your own kin — who, whilst *I* have been away fighting the French, has been giving *them* coin to pay *their* soldiers whilst avoiding the taxes to pay our own?' Giles spat his words out with more venom than he had intended, but it had been all he could do to walk out that night and not launch himself at the man he considered to be a traitor to his King and country . . . his own uncle.

His father grimaced. 'He is a man who turns up late at night, then goes in the early morning. He asks questions, but gives few answers. He is not a traitor. Times have been hard, people have been without, and . . . ' He sighed as he looked at his son, as if realising his words fell on deaf ears.

'Rather than take the King's shilling, he would prefer to have the Emperor's francs!' Giles stood square opposite the man who he had respected all his life, and saw the downcast eyes as he stared unseeingly at the metal he had been so lovingly restoring, only to gaze blankly at it as if it no longer had any importance. Giles knew then that his uncle had involved his father in the trade too. His heart sank. What of honour and loyalty? Could any good man be bought for the short-sightedness of a quick monetary gain?

'He minds his own business. He rides the tides. Why don't you join me here?' Hopeful eyes met his. 'I mean, *really* join me here, and take on the forge after me. You are already quite competent and strong.' He stopped hammering, and Giles realised he was about to break his father's heart . . . not in vengeance for the betrayal he felt at their dealings in contraband, but because his father had many years left in him, and there was only a good living for one man — not two — in these parts. One solution would be to convince his father to move away, nearer a town whose forge was not so remote. Giles realised he might have to find his own way, his future, and ask his father to follow him, leaving the family forge that his grandfather had set up. When the soldiers were at the fort, there was plenty of work, but now . . .

Giles stood straight, trying to clear his head; for first he must find Ruby May, know her secret, and help her before his captain returned.

'Father . . . I . . . ' he began slowly.

The hammer struck hard.

'You've been through a lot, Giles. Think on it. I can see that you are in no mood to discuss it now. Your uncle will be back here tonight. Make yourself scarce if his presence so offends you.'

Crash — the hammer hit hard again.

Giles nodded and walked out. If Uncle was coming, then he would find out what the man was up to now all seemed settled after Waterloo. There was an upsurge in smuggling again, as too many sailors had returned to find little or no paying work. The comparatively new Preventive Waterguard, who patrolled the coastline in cutters, made it more difficult for smaller vessels to ply the trade — but now ingenuity had made progress in the ways of goods being concealed and transported.

He passed by the wagon that his father had been doing the work on. He looked over the centre board, glancing up to the box seat and the tail board. It was solid and well used, but looked in good condition.

'Giles, if you're going to stay around here, I'll set you to work. Or, if you fancy a walk, you can take this up to the Hall for me. Give you time to think on my proposal.'

'I'll take it.' Giles took the mended fork with enthusiasm.

'Good. Clear that head, and realise that people here make a living in hard times as best they can, whilst fat politicians cause wars and grief. Where are all the jobs now for all the returning soldiers and sailors, eh?'

Giles stepped away. He did not answer. Men had left as soldiers, killed others, and were expected to return to the life they had before. He knew many couldn't as they were damaged in mind or body, and often had no work to be able to feed the families they had had to desert.

'Think on it, Giles. Who gets fat, and who gets killed — and for what?' his father shouted after him.

Giles shouted back one word, without stopping: 'Freedom!'

9

Ruby's mind, like the last week, had been very troubled. It was Sunday, and she was expected to attend the church service with Maisie and the footman Benjamin Brandon — in the company of Cook, of course. They would sit at the back on a bench seat. She didn't care for Brandon; he had a superior air about him which was far from friendly. He was tall and handsome, in a chiselled-chin sort of way, but he had a habit of looking at people from the corner of his eye, rather than straight on, that disturbed her. Mind, she had only met him twice before. He rarely came below stairs; instead, the upper house maid, Elsie Battle, took up his meals and saw to the master. Ruby had little experience of service, and even less of life in a household such as this, but one thing was certain: this Hall ran to its own set of rules. Mrs Grambler seemed to be the link between the upstairs and down.

Mr Sedgwick had his own private pew. He entered the church at the side of the building and took his seat in a boxed pew that faced the altar and his maker's representative on earth. It was different — very different — to the bare benches that filled the convent when they were called to prayer. There had been no nooks or crannies there, nowhere to hide or skulk. When he attended, Brandon had to stay with his master to escort him safely in and out of the coach. Ruby suspected the man was fragile and old as he did not stand tall. He slumped in the pew under his hat. Well, he had on the few occasions she had been able to see him.

'Maisie, will the master be going today?' Ruby asked. If she could dawdle behind Maisie, she might be able to sit on the end of their pew; then she would be able to look across to Mr Sedgwick's with a clearer view.

'Nope, that is why Mr Brandon will be able to enjoy the service in our company, on his own for once,' she said; and smiled, but did not look down at Ruby.

Ruby almost sighed. Surely Maisie was not going to try to flirt with Mr Brandon in the church? The woman had no shame.

Ruby pondered as they stood together in the narrow stone corridor just inside the kitchen door, waiting for Cook and the footman to appear and lead them down the long winding drive to the ancient building at the end of the lane. Other villagers would arrive from up there where the village sprawled out towards Tilbury town.

There were a few who would arrive by wagon or horse, and even some by small boats landing at the fort's jetty. Ruby's imagination wandered again as she pondered how she would give anything to be able to ride the waves — well, drift along on the current in one of the fine tall ships she had watched. It was true that there were evil traders amongst them, dishonest men whose loyalty to their king and kinsman could be called into question, as well as sentenced criminals who were being taken away in chains to lands she could only imagine. Yet the desire to go and see those far distant lands as a free person was her dream. She had been kept inside strong, safe stone walls throughout her young life. An uneasy thought crossed her mind: was she not even now being kept so? Ruby knew that notion had been haunting her since the stranger arrived and somehow violated the new sanctuary she had been told to consider as her home. She shrugged her doubts away, and desired more than ever to walk by the fort and stare out at the busy river trade, letting her imagination run with the flow of the tide. Perhaps her father could arrive by boat. She kept trying to picture him — tall and dark, or maybe more her colouring?

Maisie looked down at her — literally so, as the girl was much taller — but also in the other sense: her opinion of her own importance was high, and that of Ruby apparently low.

Ruby ignored her condescending stare and continued to ask her questions. 'Why doesn't Mr Sedgwick have a butler?'

'Because he has Mr Brandon instead.' She looked away, tapping her foot impatiently.

'Yes, I know that, but that is why I am asking. Shouldn't a gentleman have a butler, and a house such as this, a housekeeper?' Ruby persisted.

'Shouldn't a lowly scullery maid just stop asking so many questions?' Maisie replied, looking back vexed toward Cook's room.

Ruby's eyes narrowed. She was not a scullery maid! Mind, she really didn't know what maid position she held, for all she did was obey Cook's bidding: be it to fetch, carry, wash, or run errands to the stableyard or gardener. Dismissing such a problem as unimportant, as she was still better fed and warmer in her new clothes than ever she had been in the care of the nuns, she persisted, not wanting to be brushed off so easily. 'It just seems odd. I thought that all gentlemen had butlers.'

'No, they don't — not if they don't want one!' She looked back down at Ruby. 'Anyways, though it's none of your business, for your information, he actually did have one once.' She snapped her words out, and then annoyingly fell silent.

Ruby thought that the chance to possibly share her knowledge and gossip would be too great a lure for Maisie to ignore.

'Honestly, Cook insists we're to be ready, and then takes so long herself . . . as if we haven't got enough to do when we come back here.' She sighed loudly.

'I have the afternoon off,' Ruby said; and then, when she saw the way Maisie's head whipped around, wished she had kept her mouth shut on the matter.

'Aren't you the lucky one!' Maisie barked out her words. 'Not been here two minutes, and getting time off here and there. Weak, that's what you are. Can't do an honest day's work.'

Ruby swallowed. 'Weak?' That was not a word she would ever have associated with herself — certainly not in character. 'When did he leave?' Ruby asked innocently, ignoring Maisie's outburst. The woman blew like the wind in any direction. Thinking of the wind made Ruby's desire to be outdoors, instead of stuck in a stifling corridor with Maisie, even greater. If only she could wait in the garden where she might see someone other than her petulant companion and Cook. One person came to mind: the handsome face and strong physique of the local hero, Giles. Was her father a hero, like him? He might have had to desert her for a higher cause.

'Who?' Maisie looked at her, either puzzled or still angry; it was difficult to tell with her, as her face was so often screwed up in some expression of disgust or distaste. However, if a delivery was made to the house, no matter how scruffy the delivery man was, Maisie would smile at anyone in trousers. Ruby realised that, as time passed her by, Maisie was out to catch herself a man before it was too late. Fine chance, she thought, in such a lonely place as the Hall.

'The butler . . . ' Ruby had been quite happy picturing Giles, and nearly said his name by mistake. How odd! She felt a rush of emotion sweep through her body. Whenever she thought of him, she experienced the strangest of reactions — and they were pleasant. Her head was filled with notions of being with him, wondering what it would be like if he touched her — or she him. The sisters would have doubted her moral fibre, but Ruby did not doubt that the fibres of her body were in tune with those of her soul. She found Giles attractive, and in his eyes she saw a man she could trust.

'Oh, him; well, it was before we were

blessed with you . . . a good few months before.' Maisie was now looking at her strangely. 'As it happened, the housekeeper left a month or so before him. We were told by Cook that she would not be replaced, but that instead herself and a new upstairs maid would see to those chores. It is a bit odd, but when you're busy you just keep on believing what you're told. 'Tis best not to question what is not your business. Then you stays out of trouble. You should try it.' Maisie stared at her directly. 'Do you know something? Something that I've not been told?'

Ruby thought there was likely to be a great many things that she knew that Maisie had never had been told or shown, and therefore never been given an opportunity to grow beyond her place in life — but not about the staff's past or present in this intriguing place.

'I have never heard of them before, which is why I asked.' Ruby shrugged as if it was of no concern to her.

Maisie sniffed. 'Well, if it's odd, Cook

would know about that, and she's said naught to me, so all must be well. It must be just one of them things.' She held her head up. 'The trouble with gossip is that it leads you into trouble, so stop your meddling before it gets you into some.'

Cook bustled up to them, slightly flustered. 'Come on, girls! No use standing around and being late for the good Lord, is there?' She pushed past them and walked outside. A disgruntled Maisie and thoughtful Ruby followed on. Mr Brandon was already closing the door of the coach in the stableyard. Ruby strained to see if she could catch a glimpse of Mr Sedgwick, but he was sitting back in the seat, and so it was only his hand that she saw as the door was closing.

'Come on, dreamer!' snapped Cook, as Ruby had stopped to gaze.

Without waiting for Mr Brandon to set off, Cook led them along the narrow path that crossed the grounds and came out from behind a big hedge opposite the church. Meanwhile, the coach trundled down along the drive.

When they stopped to cross the track to the church, there was no longer any sign of it.

'Shouldn't the coach be here by now, Cook?' Ruby asked.

'You are always asking questions,' Maisie rebuked her, looking up at Cook and then at the sky in a despondent gesture.

'No, he is attending a service in Tilbury; and so we shall see to our own souls and stop minding the business of our betters, Ruby!' Cook stared at her. It was a look that thinly cloaked a warning, but then her countenance changed as her face broke into a warm smile when Reverend Hargreaves stepped forward, also looking curiously along the lane.

'So, are we not to be blessed with Mr Sedgwick's presence again?' he asked Mrs Grambler.

'Afraid not, sir; he must away today, but sends his condolences. Still, you

will be away yourself soon, I understand,' she commented, and Ruby
noted a look of surprise on the priest's
face.

'Do you?' he asked, but his eyes were
watching Ruby.

She chuckled, and then said, 'Oh,
look at the time on that there clock.
Can't have you late, can we, sir?' She
looked to Ruby and then Maisie like a
mother duck collecting her ducklings,
and added, 'We mustn't keep his
reverendship waiting; come along, girls.'
She nodded to Reverend Hargreaves,
and almost pushed them along and into
the pews at the back of the church.

Giles was already seated across the
aisle two rows down. He was with a
very strong but smartened-up man that
Ruby realised had to be his father. The
man held his back straight and looked
proud as he sat next to his son. There
was a resemblance between them that
was quite striking. When Giles looked
over his shoulder and glanced their way,
Maisie smiled and tilted her head coyly

111

at him. Ruby smiled slightly at her, but when Giles' mouth returned the gesture, she realised he had thought her humour at Maisie's reactions to be a friendly gesture towards him. When she saw Maisie beam at him even broader than she had at first, it was all Ruby could do not to laugh out loud — she had obviously taken Giles' smile as a response to her own.

The slap on her leg stung as Mrs Grambler's hand struck, and Ruby's smile disappeared. Instead, she looked straight ahead: it hurt her pride as much as her skin, but she would not crumple like a child and pout. Instead, she picked up the Book of Common Prayer, and found a page with words that spoke to her.

There was a mystery here, Ruby thought. One that involved the master, Cook, Brandon, Elsie Battle, and her missing father. The last word filled her heart with hope and joy: a father — she still had one! More, though, it all somehow involved her, and she knew not how. She stared at the words before her: 'Ask, and it shall be given you; seek, and ye shall find; knock, and it shall be . . . '

Daring to glance up again, she looked across at Giles and his father, who were now both looking forward as the service was underway. Perhaps Giles, as the other outsider to the area, could be of help to her. He too had been away, and so might offer her a friendship that could aid her in revealing what was going on. He loved his father — he would understand her situation. Something made her certain of it. If only she could speak to him alone — but how?

10

The service ended and the church emptied of its flock. Cook stayed outside, apparently trying to be discreet as she caught the attention of Flora Sessions. Meanwhile, Maisie was hanging back, chatting to the widow Hemmings from the village bakery and her son Jebediah. He was a strong, well-built man who worked a piece of land left to them by his father; but he was not the brightest button on parade, Ruby thought, as she had heard Cook say so many a time in the kitchens. If Giles was agile like a thoroughbred, Jebediah was strong like a shire horse. However, Maisie didn't seem to care if he were agile of body or wit. He was not bad in looks, had property and offered her a chance to still find a husband.

Ruby was looking around for Giles

Marram. He seemed to have disappeared. She longed to share with him the mystery of the stranger in the house. Why she should trust Giles, she knew not, but she had to trust someone. Cook was always so dismissive of any questions about Mr Sedgwick and the reason why she was brought there. Maisie had only her own ambitions in mind. No servant talked to her openly. Mr Brandon was as elusive as his master and the upstairs maid/ housekeeper person did not venture down to mix with them.

'Hello, I do not believe we have been introduced,' the Reverend Hargreaves greeted her with a voice that flowed as smooth as honey. It was familiar, and yet so filled with the tone of his class — the education that removed any regional accent in favour of a uniformed way of talking — that it could have belonged to any or rather many gentlemen. Not that she was an expert in the subject; but, other than the Irish priest who had visited the convent, men of the cloth inevitably all spoke in a similar tone. She had listened to them as they preached, as was her duty, but the words had begun to glide over her, their lessons repetitive and lost as she instead chose to discern the speakers' tone, rhythm, origin, or health. It had broken the tedium.

'No, sir, we have not. I am Miss Ruby May Tranton, recently moved into the Hall's service.' He had a pleasant smile and eyes that she thought showed a quickness of wit.

'Well, Miss Tranton . . . Tranton. How are you finding life at the Hall?' he asked, with a half-smile playing on his lips, as if something humoured him.

'Pleasant,' she replied, thinking it an odd question for a priest to ask a maid.

'Not too arduous, then?' he persisted, and the smile crossed his mouth.

'No . . . not at all,' she answered.

'Tell me, are you any rel- . . . ' His head turned sharply as Cook's voice broke in. The apparent good humour instantly left his expression to be replaced by one of indignation.

'Ruby, go on back to the Hall. No use idling around here,' Cook abruptly interrupted their conversation without any apology to Reverend Hargreaves. 'I think Mrs Hemmings is wanting to see you, Reverend. Excuse us, I must get these girls back to their duties.' She took Ruby's elbow and walked her down to the lychgate without awaiting a response from the priest.

'But I have the afternoon off . . . ' Ruby said, as Mrs Grambler stopped by the gate and gestured to Maisie to make her way over to them. Ruby glanced back and saw Reverend Hargreaves still watching her. He was standing facing them, tall and rooted to the floor, despite Mrs Hemmings talking to him.

'What was it he was going to ask me, Cook?' Ruby asked.

Cook stared at her. 'How should I know that? I am not a mentalist. Yes, you lucky girl, you have the afternoon free, so do not waste it gossiping like you've nothing better to do . . . And with the vicar, too!' She shook her head, as if Ruby had somehow sinned against the social order of life as she understood it. 'So go back to the Hall and spend it reflecting on your good fortune, young miss.' She gestured that Ruby was to scurry along.

Annoyed at being so summarily dismissed, Ruby walked back up the path to the Hall a ways; but stopped and instead headed through the walled garden, aiming to cross over the field the other side of their estate and go on further to explore the small village that lay beyond, in particular the black-smith's smithy.

'Wait up!'

Ruby spun around just outside the entrance to the walled garden. A hand cupped her elbow, and she was pulled behind a yew hedge between the red-brick wall and the mass of dark green branches. Ruby was about to kick her assaulter's shin when he moved his leg quickly to the side. Her leg swung through empty space, before being swiftly clamped between Giles' thighs as he swung her back to the wall, pinning her there.

'I'll scream, you brute!' she snapped, wondering why she should ever have trusted this man. As if he could save her from whoever had appeared in the Hall when he behaved in such a brutish way!

'That would be folly. Now, promise you will keep that booted foot firmly on the ground, and I will release you.' He opened his eyes wide at her, waiting for her assent.

For a moment, she hesitated — the thought, surprisingly, caught her off-guard as his body was so close to hers. It provided more comfort than a blanket on a cold winter's night. There was a strong sensation of pleasure growing from the initial rush of fear when she had realised who it was. She relaxed her body and nodded.

He smiled back at her. 'Good.'

Ruby tried hard not to respond in any way, taking only the shallowest of breaths as he stepped back.

'I am sorry that I surprised you in such a direct manner. However, you were crossing the countryside at such a pace, I thought you were a woman driven on by an urgent mission. I did not wish to shout out and alert any straggling parishioners that I was chasing after you.' He stood, casually resting one hand on a branch above their heads, still temptingly close to her in their own dark secret hollow.

'Why were you chasing me?' she asked.

'I wanted to talk with you — alone,' he explained, tilting his head to one side.

'Why?' she persisted, wondering if he was in fact capable of reading her mind.

He looked out beyond the branches, but there was nothing and no one to see other than open country and a river beyond the marshes.

'You know, Ruby, I am only recently returned here. You are new here also, and I am curious about many things that have changed since I grew up in this small part of our beautiful land: things that, in some way, may relate to your sudden appearance here.'

Giles was serious, she could see that.

She stood straight. The words he spoke to her made sense. But they would not have, had it not been for the arrival of a stranger who had spoken to her inside the Hall. So who was he? Why had he been there, and what else involved her? Giles had grown up here, and yet he felt as if his home had changed. There was something very wrong. Both knew it, so her only hope was to trust him — or perhaps she wanted that to be the case. The vicar had been about to ask her something when Cook had intervened, so perhaps she was placing her trust in the wrong man. Should she be going to see him instead?

'It is just that I am not sure why you should think I am involved in the changes in some way. I was brought here to work in this house from the convent where I was raised. I have not seen the master yet, but Cook said that he is reclusive and we all need to respect his privacy.'

She looked away.

'Who are you?' he asked, leaning a little closer in to her.

'Miss Ruby May Tranton . . . ' she replied, his face so tantalisingly close to hers she could feel his breath on her cheek.

He stood back slightly, as if he needed to lose the distraction of glancing at her lips as she involuntarily licked them, her thoughts split between the spoken word and the feelings stirring deep within.

'I know that, but who is your mother? Who was the man you call Father — or who should carry that honourable place in your heart? Why and how did you end up at a convent? Which one were you raised in? I do not know of one that is so near that it would provide a maid to a Hall in such a backwater as this; and yet you are not treated like a normal scullery maid, are you?' He rested his hand gently on her shoulder for a second and then removed it. His touch, the intimate gesture, had not scared her. She had liked it, but the questions still ran around her mind, upsetting her as there were few answers she could give him.

Ruby was slightly taken aback that he should be so forthright, yet his thoughts were mirroring her own. 'I work . . . '

Giles took her hand in his rough one, and ran his fingers across hers and then onto her palm. The slow movement as he stared into her face made her swallow.

'These hands have not been made to scrub floors and pans, or do laundry for endless hours on end. They are soft and tender as your heart, Ruby May. You are not working here as a maid, but being kept here — why? Have you any notion as to the reason?'

They stood holding hands, staring at each other. Ruby wanted to deny his words were true, but they were. She had been given lighter chores than

Maisie, which was one reason why the girl loathed her. She suspected the other was that Ruby was more delicate in looks than her.

'You are scaring me,' Ruby whispered.

'No, Ruby.' He tenderly brushed a wisp of hair away from her cheek. 'It is not me that scares you, is it? But the truth in my words.'

11

Ruby pulled her hand away. 'Look you can ask me anything you wish, but I have no idea where my parents are — *if* they even are, that is. All these years I have thought them to be dead, but that man told me my father would come to me . . . ' Ruby was about to step outside the shadow of the trees and into the daylight when she saw Cook coming around the corner of the lane. She was busy talking to the widow Sessions.

Giles put a hand on her shoulder, pulling her back further inside. 'Stay in the shadows. Those two are up to something. The way they are talking, they are as thick as thieves — I use the word literally!' He placed a protective hand on her shoulder.

'I do not like being a shadow person, Giles — my place is in the sun and in the light of day.' She looked up at him, but did not twist away from his gentle yet firm grip.

'You will be. But there is a need for shadows in everyone's life at times, or else how would we know when we fell the full warmth of the sun? Be patient, little one.' He gently squeezed her shoulder.

Ruby liked the way he used his words. For one so young, he seemed to have gained the wisdom of years beyond his own. Perhaps, she thought, that was the gift — or curse — of war. Childhood innocence, if not natural optimism, was lost. Yet the man could still reach out with a sensitive touch. However, it did not feel as though her time in the sun was yet at hand. But the warmth she felt from his touch was comforting, if not distracting.

'I thought Mrs Grambler was just being kind to me,' Ruby remarked. 'I thought it was because she liked me.' She snapped her thoughts back to her present predicament. She huddled next to Giles as the women came closer to the gate of the walled garden; their harsh tones seemed filled with anything but kindness.

'You can say that all you like, but I tell you, he'll have to go sooner than we planned. If he has linked that connection, then it won't be long afore he'll be over at the Hall demanding to see Sedgwick — then what'll we do?' Sessions spat out her words.

Ruby wondered who 'he' was.

'He's a busy man; he has more to bother him than a young slip of a lass who knows no better than to wander off on her own,' Mrs Grambler answered quickly, and shook her head. She was anxious, Ruby could tell. Not only was her skin doing that red flush thing around her neck, but she was wringing her hands.

'Aye, well; you keep letting her do that, so long as you know where she is when the time is right, for it will make the travelling and her disappearance a lot easier to explain. We'll need to put miles between her and him — pardon the pun,' she chuckled.

''Tis no time for humour, Flora! Shame, really, she's not so bad — but bad blood's bad blood, and if that is what we have to do, then . . . '

Cook's voice drifted off as they scurried into the garden behind the wall.

'Bad blood?' Ruby mouthed the words, not wanting to say them out loud, but realising it must be her own they spoke of. 'What humour was in her words?' She looked up hopefully into Giles' face, but he was staring out of the shadows in the direction of the two women as if he was trying to penetrate the stone of the wall and follow their conversation or meaning.

'Giles . . . what do they mean by my 'bad blood'? It is me who they were speaking of, I sense it. What is it they know that I do not?' She stepped away, her hands clenched at her sides. 'Giles, there is another mystery to solve — and I need your help, for I do not know what to do.'

'Tell me all. I give you my word that I have only your best interests at heart.'

'A strange man came into the Hall. I was in the library when he appeared — from the shadows. There must be a hidden passage other than the servants' corridor that I did not know about.' She swallowed. 'I ought not to have been in there, but the draw of all those books not being read was too much, and I wanted to see the sun go down. I gave in to temptation.'

'When was this?' he asked.

'Yesterday.'

His attention was fully on her. Ruby's heart was beating faster, because she had to trust Giles — but then, she had trusted Cook. Once she revealed her secrets, it would be as if she had allowed this man into her soul. He could protect, help, or destroy her.

'Yesterday evening. I couldn't tell Cook, for I had no right to be in there. So who was the man who appeared like a spectre?' As she said the last words, his head snapped around and he stared back at her. He took hold of her shoulders and made her face him square on.

'This man . . . What did he look like?' he asked. 'Describe him to me.'

'I don't know who he was, but he came out of the shadows of the library, and he knew who I was.' She rested her head on his chest and sighed. 'Giles, I have been a no-one all of my life — now, it seems as if people are chasing my father, and I am to be the bait to catch him. Please help me. I must find out who he is and help him. These shadow people are all around us. I cannot trust them — any of them — and I have no idea who I really am. You are the only one that I have faith in.' Her eyes were wide in both hope and fear. She saw before her someone who also knew what it was to feel like an outsider. Even if he had been raised locally, he felt the same sense of detachment and isolation as she did.

She felt him sigh deeply as she spoke. Was he moved by her words, or sensing her vulnerability and the responsibility she was placing on his war-weary shoulders? Why should he want to meddle in her affairs when he had had enough of dealing with conflict? To her relief, his arm slowly rested around her shoulders, pulling her closer to him. She felt the weight of him as he rested his chin gently on the top of her head. 'We shall do what we must to get to the truth of this matter. But you must promise me never to call yourself a 'no-one' ever again — for you are a 'someone' who is of great import . . . at least to me.'

She felt his kiss through her hair just before he stepped away.

'You are in danger, and I think the first thing we need to do is to find a way of getting you away from here to a safe place. Leave that thought with me. For now, you will return to the Hall as they expect you to.' He scratched his head. 'Raise no suspicion that you are aware they are playing a game of sorts with you. Be attentive, and if you have a chance, see if you can see Mr Sedgwick clearly when he is in the house; for there is something about this reclusive character that also rings false.'

'You are . . . sure that I am safe to return there? How will we discover more about my father unless I am here for him to find me? He must be coming for me, but who do we ask for help from if these people are part of a plan to entrap him?'

'Tell me more about this man who appeared to you. Is there anything at all that he said or did that would make you suspicious as to who he might be?' Giles was standing looking out of the yew tree's cover. His mind seemed elsewhere.

Ruby joined him at his side. 'He had a very calm manner, was tall, knew his way in and out by some hidden door in the library, and was surprised that I knew not who my father was, or what he was. He seemed to find my total lack of knowledge on the matter quite humorous.'

Giles pulled his lips together and chewed his bottom one as he thought. Ruby realised that her description did not leave a lot to go on, but then as she looked back toward the church there was something that resonated that had passed her by earlier. It was the smooth-as-honey tone, and the words of advice: 'All is for the best . . . '

'Pardon?' Giles asked her. He was understandably bemused by her seemingly random statement.

'He was not amused by my reading Voltaire. He almost preached at me for challenging my rightful role as a woman, and supporting the idea of education for my sex. Well, that was what he meant . . . '

Giles put the palm of his hand up and shrugged his shoulder. 'I'm sorry to say, you have just stated a belief held by most of the men within the nation, I suspect. So why was his comment so different from those others?' he asked, then added, 'And what were you doing reading Voltaire?'

'I found it. I have never read the man's words before, but they were most challenging and . . . different in their perspective on life.' Giles raised an eyebrow, so Ruby continued quickly, 'No, it was the way the stranger spoke to me. There was a barely hidden passion about his words. Like preaching, like he was used to putting people in their place — especially women. His tongue rolled them smoothly out — ' Ruby looked back to the church. ' — like the speech Reverend Hargreaves, who is another relative newcomer to the region. And yet, according to Cook, he is going to move on soon.'

'How does she know this?' Giles asked, his face creased in concentration as he took in the importance of her words.

'It seems she wasn't supposed to, because she let it slip, and then quickly bustled us off to church.'

'Oh, Ruby! It seems that we have stumbled upon far more than just the mystery of your parentage here. Whatever is amiss in this small backwater involves people we may know and trust — or, rather, that *I* know and trust. You will have to place your faith in me to do what I can to sort the puzzle. Please return to the Hall. I will make some more enquiries, and I will come to you early tomorrow. I will be in the walled garden near the potting shed when day breaks.'

Ruby nodded, took a step towards him, and whispered, 'Please take care of yourself, Giles. I would feel awful if my problem somehow escalated into something that involved you in danger.'

He smiled, took her hand, and gently kissed the back of it before doing a deep bow in the shadows. Standing tall again, he calmly announced, 'I fear, Miss Tranton, you have already involved me, heart and soul. Now, you go — and take care.' He took two steps back, nodding at her, before turning on his heel and making quickly away as he skirted the outside of the wall before disappearing from her vision.

12

Giles walked around the outside of the church building. He had waited for all signs of life to dissipate before making his way to the vestry door. Placing his hand on the large iron handle, Giles slowly pulled it down. Why he did not just walk into the room, he was unsure. After all . . . it was a church. It was a Sunday and, although the service had ended, he should hardly be turned away. He was a sinner, after all. He half-smiled.

Compared to the brighter daylight outside, the inside of the chapel seemed very dark. He slipped into the office-cum-vestry at the back of it and looked around. There was a large oak cupboard where the vestments would be hanging ready for their next use. Opposite was a large oak desk; and in the wall, a safe of sorts, where the sacramental vessels would be safely locked away. Giles looked down and noticed a rug on the floor that had a corner flipped up. Curiosity got the better of him, and he realised that hidden underneath it was a hatch door, presumably to the crypt.

Giles was studying the mark at the edge where the rug had lain, and saw recently disturbed dust. He paused momentarily as a strange, yet familiar, sensation swept through him. He stood up. A feeling in the pit of his stomach had told him he had been discovered.

He looked over his shoulder to see Reverend Hargreaves standing there in day clothes, watching him, his hands deep inside his greatcoat pockets. The high hat upon his head made him appear even taller than his already lofty height. He appeared to be dressed all ready to go riding, rather than to sit and have his meal in the vicarage, as Giles presumed most priests would after they had fulfilled their obligations.

'Can I help you?' he asked dryly. 'Have you misplaced something?' he added, sarcasm dripping from his tone as he glanced at the rug, which Giles had hastily flipped back down to its original position.

'Yes, on both accounts. I was hoping to catch you here, as I wanted to speak to you privately.'

One eyebrow rose. 'Really?' His voice held mock surprise. 'You need only attend the service and have a word with me afterwards, like so many of the parishioners normally do.'

'I did attend; but, unlike Mrs Grambler, I would rather talk to you as I explained — in private.' Giles kept his comment discreet, his meaning plain.

At the mention of Cook's name, the reverend's attention seemed more focused.

'Please, carry on, I am all ears — but I should inform you that I do not normally hide underneath an old rug, or in the crypt, or where it leads to.' He leaned back against the door frame. His posture seemed casual enough, but Giles sensed he was trapped — and that this man, who wore the garb of a vicar, was acting more like a trained soldier.

He had blocked the only way of escape, and Giles suspected he might even have a weapon concealed in his pocket.

'You have not been here long, I understand,' Giles began, wondering if the man did ever hide under the rug in the crypt, or conceal contraband there. He would hardly be the first priest to use the church to disguise a stash.

'Neither have you, Giles Marram, but your father and uncle have. They have been very industrious throughout the years of conflict.'

Giles registered the reference to his uncle, but let it pass as if it did not seem at all odd. Uncle Josiah lived in another parish and was hardly a regular church-goer — his sister had told him that his soul would be damned. So this newcomer had knowledge beyond the immediate villagers, and of his family's 'industrious' years. That seemed very strange and somewhat troubling. He was obviously inferring that he knew something of the nature of their business.

'I was born and raised here,' Giles

answered, whilst he turned each thought and fact over and over in his mind. What was this man? Why was he so knowledgeable about his father's and uncle's business?

'Yes.' The other man nodded. 'You were, and no doubt your tribal loyalties are strong.'

'Tribal loyalties?' Giles repeated. Reverend Hargreaves merely shrugged.

The man's words insulted and patronised him. 'We seem to be losing the point of the conversation, Reverend. I heard that you are to move on soon — may I ask why? You have only recently joined the 'tribe' here.'

Giles saw surprise in the priest's face when he heard the question. 'I am unaware that I am apparently to move on.' He sounded genuine enough. 'You and I both know I could live amongst your people for thirty years, and I'd still be considered an outsider.' There was no bitterness in the man's voice, but an edge that showed he knew too well the truth of it.

'Mrs Grambler thinks you are.' Giles ignored his point. It was true enough — but then, the same rule applied to small communities the world over, or so his experience of it had showed.

'Is she the authority who dictates who comes and goes or who stays?' The reverend changed his weight from one foot to the other, still maintaining a casual stance, but Giles realised he was poised also to run or pounce should he need to.

'Not that I know of; but then, if you will not answer that question, then I will ask you another: Why would you sneak into the Hall and confront one of the maids?'

'I think our audience has come to an end, Giles Marram. Either the heat has got to your brain and addled your wits, or you are a very jealous and possessive man who suspects anyone — even a priest who merely passes the time of day with Miss Tranton — of trying to get in your way.'

Giles stood straight and nodded as

both men realised Reverend Hargreaves had made a fundamental mistake. Giles had never said *which* maid the Hall's invader had confronted.

Hargreaves also stood tall. His hand emerged from his pocket clutching a small pistol, which was trained on Giles' torso. 'Now it is time for me to ask some questions of you, and your turn to answer them. For if you do not, you will find that a spell in Tilbury Fort as a traitor will glean some worthwhile answers, of that I can assure you.'

'Me! A traitor? It is you who has had his wits addled. I have just come back from serving in . . . '

'Spain, yes, I know. You were caught, taken to a French jail, kept there as a prisoner of the Emperor — as he liked to be called — and yet you miraculously escaped . . . along with your captain, after destroying a ship of France by your sole effort.'

'Who or what are you if not a priest, sir?' Giles realised this man was either a well-informed spy, or in some other way was working for the government. Either option left Giles in a very awkward situation. What had his father and uncle got themselves mixed up in whilst he was away?

'I am a priest, yes — and a soldier — and a loyal subject of my country. Unlike your Captain Miles.' The man's lips set as he snapped out the last unpalatable words.

Giles took a small step back. The widow Sessions, he realised, had made a pun of the name. Of course — 'put miles between her and him'. The captain was the father who so desperately wanted to find Ruby . . . his daughter? But why did that make him a traitor? It just made no sense. It was no crime to sire a child out of wedlock. Morally, perhaps, but not legally. But how could this involve someone like Hargreaves?

'You have my attention, sir. I know nothing of what you speak. Captain Miles cannot be a traitor, surely. He negotiated my release . . . he did not desert his men, but worked with another officer whose family had raised funds to secure it. He was always loyal to his men . . . ' Giles' words trailed off as Hargreaves shook his head and sighed.

'You really believe that? Or was it mainly to this one?' He pointed to the man who had been the young sergeant promoted on Miles' request. 'Convenient, really — you were just where he needed you to be so that he could keep a close eye on you, and make sure you returned safe and well. Oh, and let us not forget, indebted to him also. Someone he needed to use to gain access to a treasured belonging he had left behind many years since — his precious gem, a Ruby.'

'I do not see how he would know that. Ruby has not been here as long as I, and therefore he could not have foreseen her arrival.' Giles' mind was humming with Hargreaves' words. They rang true. But why had he not seen through Miles before?

'Could he not? Not even if he was working with people here to arrange it?' Hargreaves stared at Giles as if willing him to see, to acknowledge, the light — the truth — in his words.

'Why here? Why me?' Giles was genuinely bemused.

'Someone wanted you safe, Giles. Someone here who had revealed his daughter's existence to Captain Miles. He wanted you back here — a life for another life. Secrets shared and a life saved.' Hargreaves raised his left eyebrow.

Giles grimaced. His father or his uncle was involved — maybe even both of them. He realised he had to tell the man the truth. 'He will return in six days. He will have me confirm that Ruby May is the woman he seeks. He has a small portrait — a miniature of a woman who looks amazingly like her.'

'Yes, he does. It is of her mother. You will go to the Bull Inn and wait to see him in this clandestine manner as you have arranged. Meanwhile, he will have his daughter taken to a launch where he will join her. She will not realise until they are crossing the Channel that she is to leave her homeland and take up a life in France. You will be arrested as a traitor who has worked within your family. Meanwhile, Captain Miles will be away, and it will appear that you have worked with your uncle to trade coin and secrets to the enemy. Miles will then be clear of all suspicion, and he will be free to return once you are shot, or hanged, to resume a respectable life with the heir to the Sedgwick estate.'

Giles stared blankly at the man. 'Who?'

'Miss Ruby May Tranton, the daughter of Mrs Amelia Tranton, and officially the daughter of Mr Reginald Sedgwick, owner of Yew Tree Hall and his associated estates in the colonies. Miles is her real father, however. Amelia and he were desperately in love, but her family made her marry a major for his wealth and position. Your captain

146

became a very bitter man. He would not accept her obedience to her father's wishes and her intention to marry the major. Miles took Amelia as his lover — perhaps by force, for she was said to be an emotionally troubled individual, and hence unable to raise her own child. She only ever had the one baby.

'A letter that Miles wrote to Amelia was discovered at the Hall by the cook. The details of what happened to Sedgwick and Amelia are unknown. But I aim to find out very shortly. The cook realised that the lady of the house must have declared the truth to Miles — that he had, in his moment of raw passion, given her a child, but stolen from her the chance to give her husband sons. However, you are a pawn in a much bigger game of chess than you can imagine. Ironically, his daughter is completely ignorant of all this.

'So, Giles Marram, you can follow your captain like a devoted puppy and end up starving in a kennel; or you can be a faithful hound, work for the security of your country, and put this man in a place he has belonged for many a year — hell. He has been the cause of several good men's deaths, and I will not stand by and let the bastard escape justice. So, tell me — are you a puppy, or a hound who is in on the chase? The choice is yours.' He raised his pistol and aimed it directly at Giles' heart. 'Are you a hero or a traitor?'

13

Ruby returned to the Hall. She slipped past Cook and Flora Sessions as they talked by the fireside in the kitchens. Knowing she was thought to be in the village, Maisie was taking a nap in the dairy, so Ruby ran over to the servants' staircase that would lead her to the passageway between the library and the master's study.

Ruby had not taken long to decide that she was not going to sit by for goodness knew what purpose. No! She was better than that. The man had appeared to her in the library. He was definitely not a spectre — his presence was real — therefore, there had to be another way into the room. After all, the Hall was riddled with passages for the servants. She would find it, the secret entrance, and trace the corridor back to wherever it led.

Giles might have wanted to help her. She did trust him, but she was also able to think and act for herself. Her life might depend upon it — and whoever her father was, he too was in great danger. She would save him from these people and discover the man behind the name of Tranton.

Ruby entered the library and made sure that she stayed close to the wall as she skirted it, running quickly across the room to the vantage point of the tall rectangular windows. The shutters were half-down to keep the light's rays from bleaching the spines of Mr Sedgwick's precious books. Not that she ever saw him read them — or actually saw him at all!

In the dark corner was a high-backed leather chair. It was positioned so that whoever sat in it could see across the gloom of the room by the light shining in from the tall windows opposite. She stepped behind it where a heavy curtain hung. The ancient oak panelling on the wall was plain. She looked for any obvious handle or bracket, but there was no trace of either. Ruby pushed each section of the panel, but there was no give there either. She sighed.

'If it doesn't unlatch, and can't be pushed, then it must ... ' she muttered. Then she smiled, for she realised that this panel was flush with the wall rather than raised. She squatted down and felt the edge of the panel at floor level. 'Of course, it has to slide behind the other ... '

Ruby was not disappointed when, as she leaned her weight evenly upon the panel, pushing it gently sideways, it moved back, and she was able to slip the edge behind the fixed panel to its right. That done, she felt a cold waft of air drift up. The space behind was dark. Realising her stupidity, she gently coaxed the section back into its original place. She had no lamp to light her way, and no club of any sort to defend herself with should she meet the man in the depths of darkness.

When she walked out of the library

again, heading to the upper landing along yet another narrow stone servants' passage, she realised that in her relief she had begun to breathe more easily. She knew that, come her return, she would be better prepared; but for now, if the shaking that had begun at her core could steady, she would find what she needed and carry out her mission with the same steadfast resolve she had begun it with.

★　★　★

'Do I have a choice?' Giles asked.

'We always have a choice, man. I am sure that you will choose wisely, but right now you are too valuable to me to allow you to run off and warn your father or uncle that all is not as it seems. Therefore, please pull back that mat and open the hatch. I will show you what is below, as you were so keen to find out.' Hargreaves stepped forward, but not near enough to Giles to be disarmed.

Giles stepped back to clear the way for the hatch to open.

'You will not shoot me, as I am innocent of any wrongdoing. Besides, your parishioners would be flocking back at the sound of the gun.'

'Go on, I will follow.' He gestured with the pistol that Giles should begin the descent into the darkness.

Giles hesitated.

'Man or mouse?' Hargreaves taunted.

Giles took the first step onto the ladder. He wanted the man to think he was doing his bidding, but aimed to switch his weight around so that instead of descending down the rungs, he swung his free leg, trying to knock Hargreaves' leg from underneath him. Alas, his adversary was too well trained. Instead, he felt a heavy push between his shoulder blades, and he crumpled as he fell down into the cellar below. Instinct took over, and he landed and rolled forwards, saving his ankles from breaking.

'I will be back later. Stay there and be

patient. If you decide to work with us, we may consider eradicating the charges we have listed against your father and uncle, and their cousin Flora Sessions.' Giles heard the man's words, but knew nothing of the connection with Sessions. 'If you do not, then we will arrest them all, place them in gaol, and take Miss Tranton as our security against Captain Miles.'

'She is innocent in all of this, man!' Giles shouted up. His anger at his foolery pumped through his veins, as did the realisation of his helplessness in saving Ruby from whatever fate Hargreaves had in mind for her.

'We know.' The trapdoor slammed shut.

The black was total. There was no glimmer of any light from even a crack. Giles closed his eyes tightly and opened them again, but there was no difference. It was like being smothered in a blanket of ink. He swallowed. He did not like being trapped in confined spaces, but here the walls could be near him, or yards away. All that broke the deathly silence was the drip . . . drip of water in the distance. The place smelt of damp rock.

He stood up slowly. There was no knowing if this was a stone carved crypt with arched ceiling, or a roughly hewn cellar. If the latter was the case, he could walk into any outcrop of rock, and fell himself like a young tree.

'Think!' He snapped the order out to shake himself from his dismay and fear. Ignorance fuelled fear, making it real. The not knowing was what triggered the imagination to steer the person to run or fight. There was no adversary here that he could openly fight, just the bleak outlook of total darkness. Yet he had to find the strength and courage to escape. Ruby May was depending on him to help her. The thought made his heart ache. He had made a promise, so he must find a way out.

He stumbled forward, retracing his fall, to find the end of the steps that led up to the hatch. It would be an arrogant man who left it unlocked, thinking that his prey would never bother trying to open it again. Unfortunately, Hargreaves was not that arrogant. The wood did not move as he pushed fruitlessly against it, and he had no choice but to drop back to the cellar floor.

With his feet planted firmly upon the rough ground, Giles regained his balance. He stood with his back to the steps and closed his eyes. 'Think!' he said.

He knew the position of the hatch in the vestry, and therefore the shape of the church above. Did that help at all? 'No!' he shouted, then pulled his annoyance back under control. He balled his fists, panic rising within him, though he desperately needed to stay calm.

'Ruby, I'll find a way,' he promised. Breathing deeply, he tried again. 'Think!' Which direction would he have to walk to get from the church to the fort? No, why would there be a tunnel from the church to the fort? It had been built years later. No . . . then an earlier building . . . of course, the Hall . . . If there was a tunnel, it would either lead to a landing place by the river, or to the nearest building of note — the Hall. Hadn't Ruby said that Hargreaves had appeared to her from the corner of the library? It was a wild guess, but it was all he could think of going with.

'Very well!' He smiled. *Try again*, he thought, and took a deep breath. He pictured where the vestry was — where in the church, and the distance it was from the Hall. Rock permitting, a tunnel would be cut directly to the place it was going to. Giles turned as if he was a compass and the Hall was his magnetic north. He stepped out slowly in that direction, and continued to walk carefully and slowly ten paces before he touched an earthen wall.

Feeling a mixture of slight relief that he had something solid before him, and disappointment that he had not rationalised the perfect escape on the first time, he took a moment to calm again.

'Think!' He felt along the wall's surface and took four side-steps to his right. There was no sign of the earth, or wall, giving way. 'Very well,' he muttered, and carefully took four measured side-steps back to his left.

'Try again,' he muttered to himself. Hes then ventured the same distance the other way. 'Three . . . ' he said, as he counted each step in turn, and was rewarded by the feeling of a cold draught on his left cheek. He stretched his hand further along the wall and was delighted when it fell away. Standing with his right hand on what seemed to be the opening to a pathway, or tunnel, he reached over with his left hand and found where the wall began again. 'Yes!' He was standing square on to an opening. Then he felt above his head, and sure enough, at the height of his forehead there was a rough arch. It seemed he had found a tunnel or passageway. Staring blindly into the depths of blackness, Giles breathed in the cold damp air, and began taking each step carefully in time with his hands following the wall on either side, so that he would know straight away if he came across a tunnel, or the opening to another room.

'Ruby, I'm coming,' he said, and forced a smile onto his face as he began counting each careful step that he took. He must not lose his way. If he did, and this was a labyrinth of tunnels used through time and forgotten about by the locals, he might never again see the light of day — or the beautiful face of his newly discovered gem, Ruby May. He used his hands to make sure that there was no other branch off the main tunnel he was following, but as it narrowed it became obvious that this was the only one. The air became less fresh, and almost stuffy at one point, but he breathed shallowly and in a controlled way, which helped.

'Stay safe, Ruby; Giles is coming,' he said, as he dared to quicken his pace a little.

14

Ruby ran up to the landing, and paused as she realised that, in her haste, she had gone up a whole flight of stairs higher than she had done with Maisie. Peering out onto this upper landing, the rooms opposite her were unfamiliar.

'Oh!' she whispered, as she realised that she was staring at the private rooms of Mr Sedgwick. She was about to retrace her steps when a door down the hall opened. Quickly, she slipped over the corridor to open the servants' door opposite. It looked like a panel in the wall, but had a tiny button handle which gave it away. She turned it, and found herself in a very narrow room that had towels and linen stacked on a shelf. Neat rows of blankets and toiletries lined the other wall. On the lower shelf were two clean chamber pots and lamps. This was obviously the store for the upper bedchambers.

She was about to retrace her footsteps when she realised that the door into the other room was ever so slightly ajar. She tiptoed over to it, and peeped directly into Mr Sedgwick's bedchamber. She felt quite anxious about the possibility of being discovered, but the drapes were only half-drawn, and the room dim. She could hear voices.

'How should I know if he does or not?' a female voice exclaimed. The indignant tone was quite strong.

'Well, he was asking when Mr Sedgwick would be available. He has not been here more than two months, and in that time he has made it his business to nose around. I tell you, he goes tonight. Josiah will take him down to the marshes; the flow of the Hope is strong, and if he can get the tide right, he'll have him away before the warden knows he's gone. There'll be reports of him walking towards the river, but nobody will be found and no one will know where exactly he went.'

'But Benjamin ... what if he is found? What if ... he's a churchman, we can't ... '

'Don't you lose your nerve now, Elsie!' the man snapped, but then sighed.

Ruby held her breath as she saw Benjamin Brandon cross the room towards Elsie Battle, the upper house maid. What were they doing in Mr Sedgwick's room, and what were they thinking of doing to Reverend Hargreaves?

'You take Amelia her tincture as you normally do, and do not worry your pretty head about Hargreaves. He is nothing to you and me. I will ensure that you are none the wiser, and tomorrow I shall take Mr Sedgwick out, as usual, on business — ' He chuckled. ' — and we shall breathe the air again. Let the minions continue to tender their protection upon the hapless Amelia and believe the lie. We shall soon be free, my love.' His words softened, and Ruby realised the next noise she heard was that of moist lips savouring each other.

Ruby backed away. She stooped and grabbed a lamp, making sure it had sufficient oil and wick in it; then, with taper in hand, made her way as swiftly as she could back to the library.

This was rapidly becoming a mission to save the reverend from harm rather than one to rescue her father. She knew not what was occurring, but somehow, somewhere, Giles was caught up in it. She might have dragged him unwittingly into her own world of turmoil. How simple and quiet life had been at the convent. It might have been hard work at times, but her existence there had been uncomplicated.

Fumbling, with shaking hands, she managed to light the lamp, placing it carefully on the floor, then pushed the sliding door open. Her heart began to pound as she entered the corridor. What was worse, she had not gone more than five anxious paces when the panel slid back into its closed position. She let out a stifled cry, but could not scream for fear that she was not alone in the bleak abyss. The corridor ahead was cold; the walls were initially lined with old wood, but that soon ended and earthen rock ensued. The ground began to angle downwards below her feet before it levelled into a narrow corridor. She could see as far as the glow allowed, but no further. Looking at the lamp, she prayed that it would not go out.

Stifling an urge to sob, she steadily made her way forwards. Then she thought she saw something move in the haze ahead of her. But then all was still again, and she decided it was a trick of the light or dark shadows. The tunnel's walls seemed to widen slightly, making the passage less daunting. She hoped that perhaps she had found the other end. Then something definitely moved.

'Who are you?' she asked, and stopped as she made out the sleeve of a man's coat up ahead as the figure rested against the wall of the tunnel. 'Is that you, Reverend?' she ventured, trying to stop the tremble in her voice from being audibly detected.

'No, Ruby — it is I, Giles,' a shaky but relieved voice replied.

'Oh, thank God!' she said and rushed towards him, but the sudden burst of motion extinguished the lamp and darkness fell around them. Giles' arms enveloped her, stopping her from falling. 'No!' she shouted, and sobbed like a child in his arms. 'I'm so sorry, Giles, I . . . '

He kissed her on her cheek and held her close. 'We're safe. We're together. You know how to get in here, and therefore we know how to get out.' He kissed her tenderly again, and she was grateful for the warmth, contact, and affection that burned through the cold air into her body.

Snapping out of her thoughts, and her pleasure at this new reassuring bond that they had formed, she had to break the magic of the moment. 'You're wrong, Giles. The door closed behind me and I don't know if it is safe to go back. We'll escape by your tunnel,' she said hopefully.

'No, that is not the answer. It leads to the vestry in the church, but I was placed down there by Hargreaves. He works for the government in some way, Ruby. This is a nightmare we have walked into. You are my dream, and I would protect you, but there is danger all around us. There is much I need to talk to you about, but not here.' Giles tried to hold back the bitterness he felt against Hargreaves, and his anger at his own stupidity for allowing himself to be entrapped.

'We have to warn him of an impending threat,' Ruby said. 'There is a plan to hurt him, and it is Brandon and Battle who are at the heart of it!'

Giles let out a long, slow breath. He was trying hard not to allow the panic he felt at the close blackness that engulfed them to rise again. Then her words struck him as odd.

'I cannot see how Brandon and Battle are involved. I mean, what have they to do with your father or Hargreaves?' He was still holding her tightly.

'They have Amelia on some kind of medicine; and they talked about getting rid of Hargreaves, as he asked too many awkward questions about Mr Sedgwick. But before I can save Father from Hargreaves, it seems that I must save Hargreaves first — and yet he has left you down here to . . . well . . . I am so confused and frightened, Giles. What is to become of us?'

'We go back to the Hall, as I cannot be sure that I have a clear path to return to the crypt. Was the passage here straightforward?' Giles asked.

'Yes, but the door closed.' Ruby sounded frightened, her voice shaky.

'There will be a way to release it.' He let her go from his grip. 'Walk back the way you came, and I will follow you.' His hand rested upon her shoulder.

He felt her straighten her back as

they slowly made their way up to the oak door. They only knew they had reached it when Ruby stubbed her toe upon it and came to a sudden halt. Giles fell into her. He quickly regained his balance, and they switched positions in the small space.

Giles meant to kiss her cheek in a fleeting gesture of comfort, but his lips found hers and, for one still, silent, magical moment, all was lost in the shadows as they kissed. Lips parted intimately; it was as if the lack of light accentuated every nerve, amplifying the feelings and absorbing them. Two could so easily have melded into one. They momentarily separated, breathing heavily, not a word spoken, before Ruby pulled away.

'Sorry,' he whispered.

'Don't be,' she replied, and kept her hand pressed firmly against his back as he moved to find the release mechanism that allowed the door to slide open again and give them both much-needed air to breathe.

15

Once free of the Hall, they had to run across the walled garden back to the pathway to the church. Standing opposite the old flint and ragstone built church, hidden from onlookers by the thick bushes at the other side of the road.

Giles studied the ancient, yet understated, place of worship. Would Hargreaves be there or had he gone elsewhere? He had no idea how much time had passed by in the tunnels; perhaps three or so hours judging by the sun's position in the sky.

Giles felt Ruby place her hand in his. He knew in his heart that he had to be honest with her as he looked down into her lovely face. 'Before we go in there and try to find the man, you must tell me what you have heard.'

Ruby did. It felt woefully little, yet the implications were stark. 'Now you tell me what you know,' she concluded.

Giles hesitated. How could he tell her that what she sought — the safety of her father — would result in his own wrongful arrest? Her father was a traitor to their country, the worst kind of betrayal. His father and uncle traded contraband, and had worked with a traitor to gain his rescue. How then to begin? Where to begin that story? She was a young maid, innocent of the world, and desperate to know the man who sired her.

Giles looked at her and swallowed; the truth might not always be what people wanted to hear, but it was best known rather than hidden. 'Ruby, we have to speak with Hargreaves if what you say is true, and warn him. However, the problem is much deeper than whatever they are up to in the Hall.'

'How so?' she asked.

'We have a traitor in our midst. One who would have me take the blame for his wrongdoings. The consequence of this is that I could lose my life. I was asked by Hargreaves to make a clear choice. I have. For if I do not do what I believe to be correct, I will have fought and killed men for nothing, for no cause that I can justify. I am sorry to be so blunt, Ruby; but I lost good men, good friends, fighting the French. And it grieves me terribly to think that someone I worked with and was under the control of — my superior officer — was feeding them secrets. The reward for my loyalty to him would be my humiliation and death.' Giles tried not to reveal the hatred he felt in all its force, for Ruby had never been near the horror of war. He hoped she would never have to experience the pure hatred and raw fear that battle madness breeds.

Ruby gasped. His words were obviously making her afraid, even though he had tried to soften them, but he had to continue.

'You will have to understand that I have to also warn my father and uncle.

They have also been unwittingly involved and named as part of the man's deceit.' He dropped his hand to his side. 'This will be the end of my world as I know it, and yet I must do my duty.' He stared across at the church. 'We must find Hargreaves.'

'Giles, whatever you do, I will stand by your decision.' Ruby looked at him. Her eyes showed tenderness and understanding as she placed her hand upon his, yet he knew well that she still had no idea about the most devastating fact in all of this. He looked down at her, and could not stop the words from slipping beyond his lips — for how else would he ever be able to look her in the face once the traitor's name was revealed?

'Ruby, my dear Ruby, the traitor is the man who claims to be your father. It is you and I who need protecting from him.'

She let loose his hand and stood straight.

'You are mistaken, Giles. Men are out to hurt him. He is coming for me . . . ' Ruby sniffed. 'Please Giles, you are mistaken . . . '

He pulled her to him and held her close. 'Believe me, I wish I was, because I served the man and thought I owed him my life — but in my heart, I now realise that he was the reason I was incarcerated in the first place. I took out a ship in harbour, but was stopped before I managed to set the supply ship alight.'

She hugged him tightly. 'That's what they meant by 'bad blood', isn't it? But is mine really tainted?'

'No, I do not believe that, Ruby. We are our own people, not moulded by some past that was not ours. You are beautiful inside and out. This man did not raise you. He may have . . . befriended your mother once . . . and that led to you, but that does not give him a claim to you as his daughter.'

'Who was my mother?' Ruby pulled back slightly and stared up at Giles, who was keeping a keen eye on the church opposite.

'Mrs Amelia Sedgwick, née Tranton,' he answered, and was surprised when she pulled away from him. He grabbed her arm, keeping her from revealing their position.

'Giles, we must go to her! She is in the Hall; Brandon and Battle have her there. They are giving her some kind of medicine. Giles, I may not be able to save my father, but my mother is here. I will know her.'

Giles held her firmly. 'Ruby, we need to think quickly. It is said that she has not been well for some time.'

A light flickered inside the church, and Giles realised Hargreaves had gone back inside. 'Stay behind me. We will go to the Hall, but first there is unfinished business here.'

He led her across the lane and into the church. The small room used as a vestry had the door ajar, and he saw Hargreaves lifting the hatch, his pistol trained.

'I have come for your answer, Giles Marram,' he shouted down into the darkness, and then stood back, waiting for Giles' weary figure to appear.

Giles placed Ruby behind the stone wall of the doorway and then answered the priest. 'I will work for my country, as I always have done.'

Hargreaves saw that he was unarmed, lowered the pistol, and nodded. 'I should have known that a war hero would find the end of the tunnel. Which one, the Hall or the marshes?'

'The Hall. You are in great danger, Reverend. It appears that there are two different plots afoot here. You may well be correct about Captain Miles. Being in the dark gave me time to see the light, if you'll pardon the pun. However, Miss Tranton has discovered that there is something odd going on at the Hall concerning the Sedgwicks. It appears Amelia is being kept there, or is ill; while the man Brandon, and the housekeeper's replacement Battle, are running the place. Where Sedgwick is, we have no idea. But it is they who are threatening to remove you, for you are becoming persistent with your enquiries as to where Miles is.'

'Good heavens! So what place do the women Sessions and Grambler have in all this?' Hargreaves put his pistol safely down and scratched his head.

'I do not know, but they want to whisk me away too,' Ruby said, and stepped into the doorway next to Giles.

Hargreaves nodded to her. 'Miss Tranton. I am sorry to meet you in such troublesome times. However, you will be very much needed to catch a traitor.'

'You wish to use me as bait?' she asked.

'Yes,' he replied.

'Very well, but so will you also be, for they want to remove you tonight. So why not leave your lamp on in here, and we shall set a trap? Once they are here, then we can go to the Hall by the tunnel, and find out what the condition of Mrs Sedgwick is.' Ruby's reasoning and level-headed suggestion had both men look at her with admiration.

Giles placed a protective arm around

her shoulders. 'This is an excellent suggestion; but Ruby, this is something we men need to do. You should be safe.'

'And where, Giles, in the nest of rats, would you say such a place might be?' Her tone was as hard as her question was to answer.

'She has a valid point, Marram. Can I suggest that your bait does what I would be doing here as a priest, and that you hide, armed, in the shadows? There are two of them and three of us. We can entrap them, and then make haste to the Hall. What do you say, Giles?'

'I say, yes!' Ruby answered. 'But there are three of them, because they said a man called Josiah would take you to the marshes and to where the river flows fast.'

Hargreaves' head shot up as he looked at Giles. 'So, where do your loyalties lie now, Giles?'

'With my country, as they always have done.'

Hargreaves nodded. 'Then we are in for an interesting evening.'

16

Ruby had reluctantly let herself be sent back to the Hall so as not to raise Cook's suspicions.

'Did you enjoy your walk?' she asked, as Ruby ran into the kitchens.

'Yes, thank you.' She smiled at her.

'Where did you get to?' Mrs Grambler asked.

'I walked towards the village, but decided it was too far. Then, when I took a rest, I fell asleep, so I crossed back and came up the lane.'

'Anyone about?' she continued, slicing a ham.

'No,' Ruby said, and stood next to her. 'The ham looks lovely,' she added, thinking of how it would taste so too.

'Have a piece,' Mrs Grambler said, sticking her knife into a small slice and holding it up for Ruby to take.

Ruby was delighted, and slipped the

ham off the blade and into her mouth, eating with relish and realising how hungry she was. Then she realised the knife was still pointed at her — as were the eyes of Mrs Grambler. Meanwhile, Flora Sessions moved out of the shadows of the arch and stood next to her.

'So, Miss Liar, what have you been up to, and with who? What have those little ears of yours been hearing?'

She turned to run, but the strong hands of Maisie held her arms behind her back, the blade now tantalisingly near Ruby's neck.

* * *

Hargreaves was, to all intents and purposes, busy at his desk. The church door slowly opened. Giles saw it; Hargreaves sensed it, and gently nodded to show he was alert. Brandon's tall figure strode in.

'Ah, Reverend. Sorry to startle you, but I had a burning question that I needed to ask you,' he said as he walked boldly in. Hargreaves faced him.

'Could it not wait until morning?' he said, and stood up.

'No.' Brandon raised a pistol. 'You see, I am so near to being free that your busybody nature is causing problems. You want to know where Sedgwick is? Well, I'll tell you. He's in debtors' gaol for a gambling debt that he defaulted on, and shall be there for another month. He lost the services of his butler and housekeeper, and I offered to help out as his wife is fragile and would never survive losing their home. His loyal staff were happy to go along with appearances. You appeared unexpectedly, as this parish was supposed to be in an interregnum, yet miraculously we are blessed with you! All you had to do was mind your flock and your own business — but no! You are a nosey one. So, you're going on a walk, and soon me and my missus will be away.'

Giles had been going to pounce upon him, but the fool was so proud of his subterfuge he was spilling the whole deception.

'So, what of Sedgwick's good wife?' Hargreaves asked.

'She's in a world of her own. Her loyal staff were prepared to cover up the subterfuge so that the family's good name could continue. When they realise we're gone, along with what we have taken out of the Hall in their fine coach, they'll look after her; and eventually Sedgwick will return, no doubt to berate their stupidity. But you will not be here to tell the tale. So, turn around, and let's make this as painless for you as possible . . . '

Brandon fell to the floor as Giles struck him hard. He then tied him up and left him gagged so he could not cry out should he rouse.

* * *

Ruby stared wide-eyed and furious at the women in front of her.

'You knew she was my mother, and

you still helped them!' Ruby spat out her words.

'Pardon?' Flora Sessions asked. 'I thought it were her father who had appeared?'

'Yes, it is, but she's also connected to the Sedgwicks in some way,' Mrs Grambler said. 'Helped who do what?'

'Trap Amelia, kill Reverend Hargreaves!'

At these words, Maisie let loose her grip. 'I want naught to do with killing, and especially not a priest!' she said, and stepped aside.

'Her wits are addled,' Flora said.

Ruby realised these women were keeping some secret, but it had nothing to do with Brandon and Battles' plans or traitors.

Ruby revealed as much as she knew. Armed with rolling pins and knives, they all descended the stairs, and faced a very surprised Elsie Battle. She crumpled into a confession. They had used the carriage to take things from the house to sell. They had enough to take them to a new life in Edinburgh, away from their troubled past. It was Mrs Grambler who struck her hard on the face, and had her bound and gagged whilst they checked Amelia. She was fragile and delicate as she always had been, and now drugged too.

'Stay with her, lass. Leave Brandon to us.'

Ruby nodded, and took the bowl of water to gently wipe her mother's brow.

$$\star \quad \star \quad \star$$

Josiah entered the church. He walked over to the huddled body that he had obviously expected to find. Without checking it was the right person, he hoisted the heavy weight onto his shoulder and made to retrace his steps to the door. Hargreaves blocked his way.

'You would murder a priest?' Hargreaves' voice accused him from the shadows.

Josiah tried to throw his burden at him, but as Brandon fell, knocking Hargreaves out of the way with a horrid thwack as his body hit the stone floor, Josiah burst out of the doorway before Giles could catch up with him. He looked as if he was going to get clean away, but a shot echoed through the night air and he fell.

Giles walked forwards. The outline of his father was something that was etched in his mind.

'Father?' he said. The word drifted across the marsh.

Hargreaves stood at his side.

'I have never been a murderer or a traitor.'

Hargreaves placed a hand on Giles' shoulder. 'Your father works for the government too, Giles. He sent word to your captain about Ruby, and instigated the subterfuge to bring him and you back here. We knew nothing of Sedgwick's stupidity and the two lowlifes that would try to profit from it. They will serve their time.'

★ ★ ★

Ruby was studying the woman who lay in bed. She had a pleasant face. Ruby poured the 'tincture' away, and gave her plain boiled water that had cooled. She enjoyed making her fresh and clean, and saw her eyes flutter open. Soon they would talk.

'She was beautiful, like you,' a voice said. A man stood in the doorway looking at her.

Ruby stood up. He walked over to her and took hold of her arm.

'My plans have changed, young Ruby, but you can still be a part of them. You must leave with me. I am Captain Miles, your father. I will explain on the way.'

'No!' she said and pulled away, but his grip tightened and she winced.

'Yes, you will, my girl, because with you there they will never dare to take a shot at me; and this night is alight with angry men who do not know their place or where their loyalties shall be.' He dragged her towards the doorway. She pulled back, and he did not hesitate to slap her across the face.

'Do that again and you are dead!' Giles had run up the servants' stairs and alighted on the landing once he had learned that Ruby had been left alone.

'You would not dare risk the life of the wench. You are soft to the core. I knew it the moment I saw you look upon the miniature. Your heart had been lost to her as mine once was to the bitch who lies in there. Learn to hate — it is less painful than to love! Now get out of my way!' He went to drag her down the stairs, but a single shot ran out and he fell.

Ruby ran to Giles, who held her like he would never let her go. To love was everything; hatred had no place in his life.

Flora Sessions walked up to the body of Giles' former captain, and kicked it with the hatred the man had spoken of.

'Love, lad, while you can; and you, girl, also. Your father and I had a brother who was cruel. He is no more. Your traitor was my lover too, but he abused me and destroyed my reputation — I had to leave my home until no one recognised me anymore.' She turned and walked down the stairs.

'Thank you — Aunt,' Giles said, trying to come to terms with the fact that she was his blood kin, and the woman smiled and nodded as she glanced back.

★   ★   ★

'Ruby, I am sorry for this.' Giles nodded to her father's body.

'So am I, but none of it was our doing. And it brought me back to my mother, and I would know her as you should know your father.'

He kissed her cheek. 'And can I know you also?' he asked.

'You already do, and shall do so more . . . in time.'

He hugged her as they walked out of the building and into a new and very different world, where trust and love could be built and deepened. Ruby held tight to him.

'To our future, Miss Tranton.' He kissed her hand.

'To our future,' she replied, and kissed his lips as he had hers in the blanket of a secret passage. But their love would no longer be hidden or darkened by shadows. It would know the light of day, and flow like the river on a course to freedom.

MOLLY'S SECRET

CHLOE'S FRIEND

A PHOENIX RISES

ABIGAIL MOOR:
THE DARKEST DAWN

DISCOVERING ELLIE

TRUTH, LOVE AND LIES

SOPHIE'S DREAM

TERESA'S TREASURE

ROSES ARE DEAD

AUGUSTA'S CHARM

A STOLEN HEART

REGAN'S FALL

LAURA'S LEGACY

PARTHENA'S PROMISE

THE HUSBAND AND HEIR

THE ROSE AND THE REBEL

We do hope that you have enjoyed reading this large print book.

Did you know that all of our titles are available for purchase?

We publish a wide range of high quality large print books including:
Romances, Mysteries, Classics
General Fiction
Non Fiction and Westerns

Special interest titles available in large print are:
The Little Oxford Dictionary
Music Book, Song Book
Hymn Book, Service Book

Also available from us courtesy of Oxford University Press:
Young Readers' Dictionary
(large print edition)
Young Readers' Thesaurus
(large print edition)

For further information or a free brochure, please contact us at:
Ulverscroft Large Print Books Ltd.,
The Green, Bradgate Road, Anstey,
Leicester, LE7 7FU, England.
Tel: (00 44) **0116 236 4325**
Fax: (00 44) **0116 234 0205**

THE DOCTOR'S DAUGHTER

Sharon Booth

After the death of her father, who had been the trusted GP of their little Yorkshire village of Bramblewick, Anna Gray decides to accept her childhood sweetheart Ben's proposal of marriage, leave her position as receptionist at the practice, and move to Kent. There's nothing to hold her here . . . is there? When Connor Blake, the new GP, arrives, along with his extraordinary but troubled daughter Gracie, Anna begins to have doubts. But how can that possibly be, when she and Ben are the perfect couple? Or, at least, so everybody says . . .

CROSSING WITH THE CAPTAIN

Judy Jarvie

Ten years ago, Libby Grant and Drew Muldoon dated for six months. Despite a string of disasters, they became engaged — then Libby broke up by letter while Drew was at sea. Now on a leisure cruise around Spain and Italy, she discovers to her horror that Drew is the captain of the ship. Can they work through their past problems and rekindle the spark and hope of their old relationship? Or will the mysterious thefts and hacking incidents on board the ship throw a serious spanner in the works?

THE LEMON TREE

Sheila Spencer-Smith

When her boyfriend Charles suggests they spend two months apart, Zoe's brother Simon invites her to come stay with him and his wife Thea in the idyllic village of Elounda on Crete, where they run a taverna. There Zoe meets Adam, an English tour guide. But business at the taverna isn't exactly brisk, and Adam will be leaving soon. Can Zoe make things work, or will she decide to return to her old life and Charles?